SKIN OF THE EARTH

WESTERN LITERATURE SERIES

SKIN OF THE EARTH

Stories from Nevada's Back Country

ART GIBNEY

University of Nevada Press
Reno & Las Vegas

Western Literature Series
University of Nevada Press, Reno,
Nevada 89557 USA

Manufactured in the United States
of America
Design by Carrie House
Library of Congress
Cataloging-in-Publication Data
Gibney, Art, 1952–
Skin of the earth : stories from Nevada's
back country / Art Gibney.
p. cm. — (Western literature series)
ISBN 0-87417-513-5 (pbk. : alk. paper)
1. Nevada—Social life and customs—
Fiction. 2. Country life—Fiction.
I. Title. II. Series.
PS3607.I26 S58 2002
813'.6—dc21 2002000641
The paper used in this book meets the
requirements of American National
Standard for Information Sciences—
Permanence of Paper for Printed Library
Materials, ANSI Z39.48-1984. Binding
materials were selected for strength and
durability.
First Printing
11 10 09 08 07 06 05 04 03 02
5 4 3 2 1

For

My parents, who endured

Joe Grikis, a lifesaver

Kay Wright, a lover of stories

The contemplation of things as they are,

without error or confusion,

without substitution or imposture,

is in itself a nobler thing

than a whole harvest of invention.

—Francis Bacon

CONTENTS

ACKNOWLEDGMENTS

The following stories originally appeared in the publications listed below:

"The Manure Spreader" in *ZYZZYVA*
"Skin of the Earth" in *StoryQuarterly*
"Wild Cow" in *Other Voices*
"Teacher's Pay" in *The Tennessee Quarterly*
"Heading for the Holy Land" in *South Dakota Review*
"A Hard Way to Make a Hundred Bucks" in *Barnabe Mountain Review*
"Water Baby" in *South Dakota Review*
"Mud Brick" in *Estero*
"The Bear Hunters" in *The Bear Essential Magazine*
"Flying to the Moon" in *South Dakota Review*
"X" in *Noon*
"Cloudshine" in *South Dakota Review*

Special thanks to Howard Junker of *ZYZZYVA,* who published my early work and has remained a significant friend and mentor.

I wish also to thank Carole Gallagher for her book *American Ground Zero,* an inspiration.

These stories are products of the imagination. The characters in them are not intended to represent any real persons.

THE MANURE SPREADER

We had three corrals, one for horses and two for cows, but that made no difference in the approach. First I piled it, starting with the horses because it was the smallest corral and the sweetest smelling. As soon as the horses saw the tractor crawling into their corral, they started running, not in a herd like mustangs, but every which way, and not because they were afraid of the tractor, but because they were happy and wanted to play. They knew exactly what was going on, because the tractor goes in the corral only once a year, in the spring, into the nearly knee-deep mixture of manure and earth, water and urine, and other ingredients, windblown, forgotten, and unseen, but still in there. When I pulled into the middle, I turned off the tractor and closed my eyes, listening to the animals pounding through the muck around me, feeling them all the way up through my seat, circling and snorting, crying out for me to begin.

All morning I moved manure. I pushed it and pulled it, scooped it and stacked it up in the middle of the corral, a huge pile by lunchtime, more than six feet high and four times as wide. The horses played on the pile like they did every year, playing king of the mountain, each one in turn standing up there still as a trophy, looking down on all the others from the top of the mound. Then I saw my father crossing the little wooden bridge over the irrigation ditch, carrying a long stick that I'd seen him use to help him walk sometimes, but now he held it in the middle and banged it against the fence posts, like he was checking their soundness as he passed. His face was yellow and waxy, and I could see the bones of his hips and knees through his jeans. By the time he reached the corral, I'd already backed out, closed the gate, and shut the engine down.

"You got the horses done," he said. I just shook my head. He knew I hated the job and that the worst part was still ahead.

"Jolina's happy," I said, pointing to the proud mare on the hill of manure.

"Been a good mare," he said, because Jolina was his mare that he had raised from a filly. He climbed up on the side of the tractor and hooked his arm around the post. I started up and we drove down to the shop, him hanging on to the side like I did when I was young. He just stood there staring out to the wind-carved hills that marked our place.

I knew a story was brewing when I saw him. He had more stories than anyone I ever met and he liked telling them, too. It didn't matter if it was just before lunch or just before bed or just before anything I'd rather be doing. He just started in and didn't stop until he was done and the story he told that day was one of the last ones he told in his life.

"Did I ever tell you about Murray the mailman?"

"Nope."

"Murray had the job of carryin' mail from Delamar to Hiko back in the days when Delamar was a mining town. He had a wagon and a team of horses he drove straight through Six Mile Valley, on the old road, around the hills to Hiko. Now,

Murray was gettin' old. He must've been in his eighties or thereabouts, but he kept on doin' it. Well, it happened that one day he didn't show up in Hiko like usual and folks got to wonderin' where their mail was and where Murray went, so the next morning a few of them rode out around the hill and found him. He was sittin' in his wagon in the middle of the valley with his head down like he was sleeping, still holdin' the reins in his hands and the horses just standing there waitin' for him to tell them to move out. He just slowed down and died right there on his mail wagon."

"Horses just standing there," I said.

"All night long," he said.

"Murray still holding the reins," I said. "His batteries just ran out."

"Batteries run out," he said, laughing. "That's good. Batteries run out just like that."

Back then, it seemed like everything that happened before I was born was just a story. And like all the stories my father told, each one had a beginning and an ending, told at different times for different reasons, pulled down from his memory as if it floated there like a balloon. Each was interesting and important by itself but had nothing to do with the others except the space they all floated in. I always thought that he told the stories only because he liked doing it, as a way of passing time or filling silence. I did not see back then that all the stories were simply snippets of a longer story, all connected just under the surface of the earth like rings of wild iris, which included me and could touch me like a long finger.

By the end of the day, I had made three mountains of manure. I saw the big bald-faced cow standing on one pile when I dumped silage in the trough at feeding time. Then, sometime after sunset, the cow got out through an old hole in the corral. I had patched the hole with baling wire years ago, but over time the wire had gotten rusty and brittle. She headed out along the ditch, over the little wooden bridge, across the cornfield and into the alfalfa, still a full month from swathing but leafy and green as she grazed out there under the moon until she started to swell. Until sometime before dawn, before the carved hills could be seen against the sky, she ate the fresh hay and finally stopped because she felt full, but it was too late. She stood there bellowing no doubt, way out between our house and the boneyard, but no one heard her as the calling pinched down to a whisper. We could not see her when she rolled over on her side and swelled until it killed her. In the morning, my father knew she was gone before I found her.

Weeds had grown up around the manure spreader in the spot I dropped it a year before, swearing I'd never touch it again. I hooked it to the tractor and pulled it back to the shop. My father was waiting with the grease gun. He kneeled down and braced his shoulder against the spreader and worked with a steadiness that was probably more for my benefit than anything else. "Calf bawlin' up there lost his mother," he said. "Big bald-face cow's gone." He pumped grease into the chopper bearings and into the bushings of the steel drum that moved the chains. I greased the square shaft, the driver—the heartbeat of the shitbox—and pulled it smoothly forward, locking it to the back of the tractor, holding it with both hands. And slowly, as each spot swelled with fresh grease, erupting from hidden spaces like wild iris, the boards warming in the sun as we limbered the stiff joints of forged steel, the manure spreader came back to life.

And then, carefully, expecting the whole cart to blow sky high, I lifted the lever below my seat and looked back over my shoulder at the square shaft as it turned slowly and turned the rusty drums and the chains and the choppers. My father gave a signal with his thumb and I bumped the throttle up a little. The spreader started rocking. With the side of my fist I tapped the throttle again and the old machine followed, striding in behind me, so I tapped again and brought it up to working speed, the diesel engine breathing and pushing, the shaft spinning, the whole contraption rocking and rocking the tractor as I sat there and watched my father move out of the way as the choppers flung chunks of old manure into the air and small stones and feathers and bits of paper and everything else that happened to fall in there.

I hopped off the tractor and stood with my father. We watched the machine, not looking for anything in particular, just looking, watching the parts move, listening to the squeaking and scraping and feeling somehow satisfied that we had done something right, that we had given life to something that had taken on a life of its own. Then my father reached up and throttled it down before turning the whole thing off.

"The chains can only give what they have," he said.

"They're old," I said.

"Everything on the place is old and wore out from workin'," he said.

"Not everything," I said. "Tractor's pretty new. And the trucks. The baler and swather aren't too old. The roof on the house—"

"The roof was leakin' and makin' streaks down the walls of the living room. We needed a new roof."

"Them chains've been breakin' every year since I can remember," I said.

"Breakin' from bein' overloaded," he said.

"They have more welding rod on 'em than they do steel they were made with," I said. "They're old."

"Old don't mean bad," he said.

"Not in people," I said. "But in machines it ain't good."

"I can spread all that manure without breakin' the chains once," he said, pointing to the corrals with his thumb.

"Take you four five days insteada three."

"Maybe *this* year you'll get a load on the field without bustin' the chains." I saw the muscles of his jaw flex and relax as he settled his weight evenly on both feet and set himself, like he set himself against a cold wind. Sometimes his determination boiled over to just plain stubborn.

I hated spreading manure. I hated smelling it, piling it, loading it, but mostly I hated shoveling it. I had to shovel it because the manure was too heavy, because I loaded too much in the spreader, not *way* too much, but just enough to break the chains that move the stuff back toward the choppers. But after feeding the horses, I got started.

The cows watched me. They waited to see if I'd push the spreader to its limit, but I didn't. "You want manure," I used to say, "I'll give you manure," and I'd load it up to within an inch of its life and pull it into the fields, but I did not say it this time. Something stopped me. It was something in the air, I think, or rather just the right mixture of many things at the right time that stopped me short. I looked over our place, across the fields to the hills and to the hills beyond them, the spine and the ribs of my whole world, where water gushed from a hole in the ground, giving water to us and everybody downstream from us, including the ducks and the geese and the fish, sending a thin streak of green across the loose brown dirt and pale green sage of that high Nevada desert. I thought of my father, a cowboy to the last drop, and the stamina he had, like a diesel engine, how he did not feel the cold as I did because he did not *look* cold or how he did not feel hunger or fatigue, because he always ate gracefully and with dignity no matter what time we sat down. He moved forward like the helmsman of a heavy ship, always taking care of everything, watching the horizon and making decisions, and we felt good because he was always in control of things. So I figured the least I could do now was to spread one load without snapping the chains, as a favor but not because I'd really learned anything.

And I pictured him gone, pictured the ranch, his empire, everything he had worked for since he was old enough to ride a horse or drive a tractor, falling squarely into my lap like a bucket-load of manure, and I swear it felt like someone grabbed me by the shoulders and shook me there in the seat of the tractor.

A few yellow birds blew in over the silo and landed on the top rail of the corral, then a few more, and then a whole flock flew in and ringed the corrals like candle flames with bright yellow bodies and scarlet heads, hundreds of them, side by side all around the rim, chirping and chattering, flitting around like fire. I figured then that something was happening, something that not only *involved* the birds and the manure spreader, my father and me, the missing bald-faced cow and the exact temperature and angle of the sun at that time, but something that could only happen once in anyone's lifetime when all those ingredients were thrown together in a way that no person could predict or plan.

The next hour unrolled like watching bread in the oven, checking on it from time to time to see that it moves closer to the only thing it can become, but not checking too often or too carefully, as the ingredients thrown together include gestures and songs and the feeling we get from very old stories and there is always something lost in the telling of it.

So I pulled the short load over the little wooden bridge and past the shop. My father saw that the spreader was not overloaded, assumed that for the first time in my life I had had sense enough to work *with* the machine instead of *against* it, even though common sense had nothing to do with it. He waved as I headed out over the ditch, not a wave hello or good-bye but just a wave of recognition.

When I reached the far corner of the field, I eased up on the lever under my seat and the choppers started spinning, throwing moist chunks of manure every which way out the tail end as I moved forward over the stubble of last year's corn. The spreader rocked the tractor down the field, pushing me as much as I was pulling it, both forces working together perfectly. I expected the chains to snap at any time, but they didn't.

I swung wide at the lower end and looked back over my shoulder. The load was half gone. I slouched into my seat and let my head roll back so the sun hit my face. There I was, gently rolling over the flat field with the tractor and the spreader doing all the work, the steady drone of the machines falling back into the distance, the sun warming me and the shit flying like crazy. It was easy. I tapped my foot to the rhythm and closed my eyes because there was nothing I could hit even if I tried and it didn't matter where the manure fell as long as it hit the field. It felt good.

When I looped around by the lower field, I spotted the bald-faced cow, rolled over on her back with her legs sticking straight up like table legs, her whole body so swollen and stiff she didn't look like a cow at all, but rather like some creature that had simply fallen from the sky and landed there in our alfalfa. I drove directly to the shop and shut the engine down, waiting for my father. "Cow's bloated in the lower," I told him as he came out carrying a long six-by-six. He rested the timber on the rail of the spreader and looked inside, saw that the box was empty and that the chains had not snapped. He looked up at me and then back at the spreader and said, "I'll drag her to the boneyard. Load up and I'll meet you." And it was there by the shop, under the cottonwood tree, leaning against the manure spreader, that he decided to die. I saw it in the way he finally looked at me, with eyes that seemed to be made of glass. He didn't need words to explain the things he wanted to tell me. He always told stories about things that *happened* or things he *did,* but never about how he *felt.* Now he was scared. And he loved me.

With his pocketknife he worked at a splinter in the palm of his hand, holding the knife like he held a screwdriver or a dinner fork, digging at the sliver of wood with the same single-mindedness he did anything. My body went numb. I scrambled for something to say or something I could do to change his mind, to deflect him, but I had done what I had done and I could only watch him remove the splinter with his knife and with his teeth and then fold the knife against his hip and slip it back into his pocket where it stayed, as much a part of him as his boots or his hat or the look on his face when he made up his mind to do something. He wrapped one arm around the six-by-six and dragged it around the corner of the shop, leaving a furrow in the dirt and leaving me no choice but to do the only thing I could do.

I raced up to the corral and loaded the manure spreader full, packing it down with the tractor bucket until the side boards bulged. My father showed up with a long chain draped over his shoulder and let it fall into the bucket of the tractor. He didn't even notice the manure spreader, didn't look at the load as he drove off toward the wooden bridge. I pulled my heavy wagon through the muck, bouncing over the little bridge, chunks of manure dropping into the ditch. I stopped to grab a shovel, because I knew this load would pop the chains.

He was waiting for me as I came around the cottonwood into the lower field. He waved at me again, smiled a simple smile of recognition. I waved back. On the back of his tractor, I hooked the chain and wrapped the other end twice around the hind leg of the bald-faced cow. My father took up the slack and the big cow started to move, scraping over the hard stubble of corn, making a hollow sound like a big canvas bag full of air, leaving a trail to the boneyard.

By the time I reached the upper field and lined up where I left off, he was halfway to the hills. I bumped the engine up and lifted the lever under my seat. The tractor started to rock, manure flying into the sun, falling in pieces on the earth, the whole pile shaking and moving slowly until the chains popped. I jumped down and grabbed the shovel and climbed to the top of the pile. From there I could see my father entering the tall sagebrush at the boneyard. As I shoveled like a madman, throwing big scoops of manure into the air, throwing another scoop before the first one hit the ground, I heard the diesel engine on the wind and imagined my father in the boneyard. Just a windless wash protected and warmed by the sun, soundless except for the occasional reconnaissance flight of a fly, the entrance is lined with the skeletons of old trucks and broken machines, guardians of the small valley, their forged bones picked clean of moving parts.

I watched my father turn and cross the ditch. He was heading for the lower field. A few minutes later, he had swung around the wallow by the cottonwood tree and was heading straight at me. I dug down through the muck and found the chains and I followed them back, looking for the break when I heard the engine noise on the wind and saw that he had turned back, heading for the wallow again. I shoveled until sweat dripped off my face onto the manure. My father was now chugging toward the cottonwood very slowly, barely lugging along, moving through the shallow water and tall grass, inching forward as if his foot had fallen off the accelerator. The nose of the tractor touched the tree, gently, without a jolt. My father sat with both hands on the wheel as if he was crossing a long valley. His eyes were not *on* the horizon but *beyond* it.

I knew he was dead. I'd known it when he had crossed the water in the wallow and I had watched him from the top of the dung heap, but it took time for me to move. The tractor pushed against the cottonwood just enough so the wheels did not spin as the tree pushed back, the forces perfectly deadlocked. Finally I could jump from the spreader and run across the corn. The manure flew from my boots as I picked up speed and splashed through the shallow water.

A sudden little wind sent his old cowboy hat tumbling backward. But he still sat with his back straight as wild asparagus, both big hands on the wheel. I took him by the sleeve and pulled him slowly onto the ground. In the grassy water, I gave him my breath. I rested and told him that I had snapped the chains. I gave him my breath again, trying to start his heart as he rocked with me in the shallow water. But he had made his decision. I dragged him out of the water, onto the stubble of last year's corn, and carried him over the field and the ditch, through the high weeds and wild iris, into the house.

For three weeks, the manure spreader sat in the field with the shovel sticking out of it, marking the spot where I stopped. It rained once for a whole day, slowing things down, washing dust from the leaves and from the shingles of our house, settling the earth into the new grave across the street. Then I shoveled manure. I found the broken chains and welded the old steel back together again. I finished up.

A white government truck came up our road. It was Howard coming to check the air machine, to change the filter and take the used one back to the test site. I've seen the used filters. When we're haying, the filters are bright green, covered with particles of alfalfa. In midsummer, when it's dry and the hot wind blows out of the south, the filters are chocolate brown with dust. In winter, the filters are clean. Howard waved to me as he pulled up under the cottonwood. He walked over with his hands in his pockets. He is a nice man, always friendly, never a bad word to say about anyone, but he isn't a cowboy.

"Howdy, Justin," he said, shaking my hand.

"Hello, Howard," I said.

"How's your dad doing?"

"Dad died. Three weeks yesterday."

"Oh, I'm sorry to hear that," he said. "Keith was a good man, a very special man."

"That's a fact," I said. "So how's the air doing?"

"Clean as a whistle," he said, like he always said, and then, "Gonna be a test tomorrow ten o'clock."

"Okay," I said. Even though the test site was just over the hill from our valley, they tested those bombs so far down in the ground that nobody felt or heard a thing.

"Any visitors?" Howard asked. "Anyone staying any length of time?"

"Nope," I said. He always asked for the names of anyone staying longer than a visit. He had the names of everyone living within 150 miles of the place, and since people came and went, cowboys and miners just drifting in and out of little outfits tucked away in canyons all through the hills, Howard had his hands full keeping the list current. We talked for a few more minutes, about the weather and the manure, and then he left. Before driving away, he sat in his truck with the engine running and wrote something in his notebook. "Ten o'clock tomorrow," he said and headed up the road for Whipple's place. The next day, I loaded the manure spreader and pulled it into the field. It was the last load of that year and the last load of my life, although I didn't know it back then.

My mother and I decided to sell the ranch that summer. She thought of raising ostriches, but I don't trust birds bigger than me and I wasn't particularly partial to cows, either. When it came time to spread manure the next year, the cows belonged to someone else and the manure belonged to someone else and I was in Sacramento working in a hardware store and going to school.

At the far edge of the field, against the hills where our water gushed out of the ground through a hole as big as a bushel basket, I hopped off the tractor and dropped down on my hands and knees and pushed my whole face into the ice-cold water, sipping slowly, feeling the force of the water surging against me as it tumbled out of the earth. I opened my eyes underwater and tried to look past the sunlight, past the loose dirt, deep below the skin of the earth, to the black lake pressed firmly between layers of smooth stone. My father had told me about the lake. It used to be above the ground. He showed me fossils of ferns in the sagebrush. He traced the shoreline with his finger as we sat on horseback in the hills, looking out over the valley in the long shadows before sunset. Then the lake slowly dried, leaving the earth shaded only by sage, moistened by occasional rain, fed by springs hidden in the hills that only my father knew. "A thing can only give what it has," he'd said. I missed him. I looked for him in the water and I understood for the first time that nothing is worse than not being alive. Even grieving and suffering are better than nothing. As I came back up, reaching the light and the air again, feeling the sun on my face, deeply breathing the warm air that blew from the west, I felt a movement in the earth, a slow rolling and a gentle but certain thumping in the ground. I thought it might be the bomb test, shaking the deep rock below the lake. I looked at my watch. It was almost eleven o'clock. Howard had said the test would be at ten. They were never late. They were always exactly on time. It was something that we all counted on. So I stood up and got back on the tractor, starting my last pass across the cornfield.

SKIN OF THE EARTH

The war was coming, so we melted into the back hills and hardly ever came down. Maybe once every two weeks we would take the truck to Carson City and load up with potatoes and dry food enough to last us. We always got stuck in a string of trucks with boys inside waving and giving the peace sign. "Victory sign, Judy," Dean would say. Then they closed the highway from Hawthorne to Carson City in the middle of the day when the trucks drove fast and the planes came over every hour. I stayed in the cabin and never went down off the mountain, so Dean drove only when we cooked the last bean and the last cup of powdered milk got lapped up by the cats. But when the aspens quaked, the government came and told us to get off the land.

Hidden away under the heavy fir trees, below the black sage and the wind, our little house leaned toward the creek. We found it one day, just like that. "I have a plan, Judy," Dean said. "A plan and the soft kiss of luck and we're home sweet home." Dean knew the way things worked. Behind the cabin somebody had dug a hole, a wide pit just big enough to sit in and stretch out. In the bottom was a rusty pick, still stuck deep in the dirt, and the handle was gray and cracked like old bone. Dean said if we made believe we were mining, the government couldn't kick us out. They wouldn't burn the cabin down if we were in it, if the cats were there and we put curtains on the windows. And it worked out just fine because that's when I started telling Dean that I'd go back to Montana if we didn't find a place to hide. I saw the war coming.

An old two-track dirt road snaked up from Charity Valley under the pines to Burnside Lake, ten miles and a trip that took our truck about an hour. The truck was old and dull and the windshield was cracked, but it ran good. They made the road during the last war to take timber and tungsten, and nobody took care of it except me and Dean. Every time we went up or down we would stop to fill ruts with rocks or build little levees to keep water under the road. From the lake, a spur road headed straight up toward the old volcano and the mine, but no truck could follow it because the snow-melt made it a creek bed. So we parked there and walked the rest, a couple minutes to the cabin.

In November the government man came. We were measuring the upper claim above the trees in the chaparral. I would pull the wire and Dean would look through his compass on a stick and he'd say up or down and then, right there, Judy, and I'd make a mark with my heel and tie a red ribbon on the sage. Then one time when I pulled the wire, I heard a voice coming from the cabin, so we dropped the wire and ran down.

The man looked funny at Dean because of his head. Two years ago, Dean got hit by lightning. He was sitting on the old volcano when it went through the top of his head and the world turned upside down and all his hair fell out. He says everything's still upside down sometimes. So the man watched us from under his faded cowboy hat and said we were in trespass, that we didn't have a mining plan and we'd have to leave. Dean held up his compass on a stick. "We're making a plan," Dean said, but the man just shrugged his shoulders. Dean told him about the tungsten mine and the tools we'd use, about the curtains and the paint, the plumbing and the road repairs. "That's the plan," Dean said. The man left.

We started storing up to stay the winter. Dean went down with the truck and I stayed and cut wood, split it, and stacked it. It scared me to be there alone when I stopped and the wind spit snow off the peaks and the clouds piled up in Charity Valley. Sometimes the planes would come by surprise and I'd run, but they came louder and lower, shaking the trees. I felt the noise on my face till they went down over the crest. Then I'd take off my clothes and sit in the creek. Dean came home and every time he'd say I had cat's eyes, wide open like a cat's when it hears something it can't see. Dean would hold me. "It's you and me," he'd say. That made me feel better.

We packed the beans away and the powdered milk and the cans and coffee. Under the floor Dean dug a hole and we put potatoes and carrots and squash down there. We let the cats live there to get mice. Dean dammed the creek with a tree, put a hose in the bottom and ran it to the cabin with a faucet by the door. With four cord outside, we were ready for the longest snow. Then, on a very cold day, the government man came back.

We were so busy getting ready for snow, we didn't have time for improvements. And that's the first thing he noticed. "We're mining," Dean told him.

"Looks like a homestead," the man said slowly. He wore an old cowboy hat, probably was a cowboy at one time because his hands were big and hard, his legs were bowed, and he didn't even move when the ice-cold wind hit his face.

From inside his denim jacket, he pulled out a big envelope and handed it to Dean. It was the papers for a mining plan that we had to file in Carson City, and pay money, before snow. "You have to show effort," the man said. "That little pit over there is the last man's effort." He pointed to the mine and the rusty pick. "And he's not here anymore."

He told us the ranger in Carson City would give us ten days to get the plan approved or the cabin would be in trespass on government land. After he shook hands with us, he left. Dean told me that since it was the cabin that was trespassing on the land, if we didn't stay in the cabin and make improvements, they would torch the cabin and burn it to the ground.

The snow was coming. Every day the sun came up on one side, the clouds came down on the other, and they met in the middle. Afternoons sizzled with snow that dropped like rain. When the clouds came, the world got small and we'd sit outside listening to the jays. They were mad. The chipmunks ran faster and the cats stayed under the cabin. Dean said, "It's coming. Even with the radio you never know." We were ready. We were only waiting. Every day Dean worked some on the mining plan papers, and we walked down to the lake or up along the open slopes below the old volcano.

One day we climbed the volcano to the top. I saw Dean put the .44 in the pack. "Why the gun?" I asked.

"Satisfaction," he said. He said one pistol can't hold back a whole world, that an army is too small, and he wanted to bring it just to make himself feel better. I said if you shoot a bear with a pistol it only gets him mad. So Dean said he would leave it at the cabin, but he pushed one flat-nosed bullet into the gun and raised it with both hands over his head, into the sun, and closed his eyes and his hands turned white around the wooden handle when he made it speak. The voice came like thunder, like waves on the beach. The jays screamed and flew from the pinetops and the voice stayed, growing as Dean let the gun down and walked to the cabin. I leaned against the red fir until the voice turned into the wind and the jays came back. Dean said, "I feel better now," and we left.

The old volcano stuck straight up out of the moss and black sage, looking smooth from a distance but really made of boulders as big as cars, stacked up five hundred feet. We climbed it like steps, the easy way from the east, and reached the top when the sun was high. The moon was in the sky too. Dean stood there with one arm pointing to the sun and one arm pointing to the moon and his head way back. "It's rare for a person to see so much at one time," he said. "It makes everything else seem so small." Then he sang his song, the one he sings every time he's happy like that.

I had an inheritance from my father.

He held the low note and looked at me until I smiled.

It was the moon and the sun.
And though I roam all over the world
The spending of it's never done.

"All ours," I said.

"You and me," he said.

We went down on the leeward side, on a flat rock hot from the sun, and took off our clothes. Dean bunched them together to make a bed and he looked up one time over his shoulder. I knew he was thinking about lightning. He let himself down, holding me, kissing my neck, and I felt the sun soften my legs and the wind on my face. Then I heard the thunder and I jumped.

"Did you hear it?" I said.

"Hear what?" he said.

"They're coming," I said.

We listened like deer, only our eyes moving. I heard it again and Dean heard it too and we spotted them, black dots above the crest.

"Bombers," said Dean.

And they were over the valley, fifteen we counted, heading for Hawthorne as we sat on the flat rock and watched them come at us on both sides. So close we could have hit them with rocks as they passed, and in the windows I saw boys waving. Some of our clothes rolled off the rock. They kept coming, shaking us in waves, and I saw Dean's mouth moving, but no words came out. Then they disappeared and the wind came back and we looked out over the valley, up the slopes of the crest, into the snow.

We pulled our clothes out of the rocks, except Dean's pants slipped into the volcano, and we walked home, Dean with his blue baseball cap and jacket, red nylon boots and bare legs. We went inside and made a fire.

The day before the mining plan was due it snowed. We ate pancakes, and after that I fed the cats and Dean worked on the plan. All day we listened to the radio. It said the war was spreading. "What if the war comes up the canyon?" I asked.

"Kill 'em," said Dean, picking up the .44 and aiming at the window with one eye closed.

"But what if there's a lot of them?" I asked.

"Kill 'em all," he said. He was serious. He stood with his legs spread, crouched down a little and fanned the hammer, swinging the gun from side to side. Then he stopped, smiled and looked at me and said, "Seven-shooter." We laughed. I like it when Dean makes jokes like that. He blew on the barrel and put the gun down.

That night we went to sleep thinking we'd be there till

spring, but the next morning there was only an inch, wet and heavy, already fallen from the pines, and the sun came through the clouds that rolled quickly in a warm wind. Dean was nervous the way he kept talking and fidgeting, getting up and down and asking questions.

"Are you sure you want to go with me to the government office?" he asked

"I never want to go," I said.

So Dean took the truck to Carson City and I stayed with the cats. He left at nine o'clock, and we figured an hour off the mountain and almost that much to town made it eleven. There'd be some talking, for sure, but lunch would put an end to that and Dean would be back by two at the latest. I sat curled up against the cabin in the sun as Dean walked down the path. Without looking back, he held the mining plan up over his head in the same big yellow envelope it came in. Then I heard the truck start, and I listened to it squeak and bump down the road until I couldn't tell it from the wind in the red fir.

All morning I made curtains. From a bedsheet I cut them and sewed them by hand, the cats watching the whole time, curled up on a towel by the stove. The radio played, and just before noon they called for snow. On old nails left by the last person, I hung the curtains, so there must have been curtains on the cabin before. I went down to the path to look at them from the outside. Curtains are small things, but they make a big difference to a house.

It was colder outside, all gray, and the blue jays kept calling as I walked up to the mine. I wondered about the last person to touch the pick because it wasn't me or Dean. It wasn't rusty back then. I tried to figure why they didn't take it with them when they left, why they took the curtains and not the pick, and I put my hands on the wooden handle. I tried to pull it out of the pit, but it was buried deep and the ground was cold and hard. With my foot I pushed on it, little by little, but I heard the handle cracking, so I stopped.

By one o'clock I knew the snow was coming, and by two I was worried about Dean. I listened for him, standing like a deer with one ear toward the road. Then I walked down to the road and listened and felt my stomach like a fist. I went back up and swept the cabin floor, opened the curtains just a little bit more, and the baby cat was clinging to the window screen, looking right back in at me, scared and crying. It scared me too, but I put both cats on the towel by the stove, and they watched me fill the firebox full and damp the stove way down. "I'm gonna get Dean," I said. But I knew by the way they looked at me, they didn't know what to think. I cleaned the sink. I lined the boots up by the door, put the cats in my sewing basket, checked the stove one more time, and at two-thirty we left. When I opened the door, it smelled like snow.

There's only one road from the cabin to the highway and only one road from there to Carson City, so even if we walked all the way to town we wouldn't miss Dean. From the cabin to the lake I walked and ran, stopping to listen for the truck, talking to the cats and running again. The lake was black, like a flat stone between the trees, and I felt the first flakes of snow hit my face. I heard the snow, sifting through the pines and falling fast to the ground. When I stopped to tie my boot, I heard the truck. "Daddy's home," I told the cats.

The engine noise cut clearly through the cold wind. But the noise came from the wrong direction, from up the road above me, and it pulled at the hill before resting and rolling in behind me. It was a green truck. It was the government man's truck, so I stopped.

He rolled down the window and turned the engine off. He looked smaller than before, about the size of a cedar fence post with his old hat pulled down above his eyes and both hands on the wheel. "Snow on the way," he said, and we both listened to it hit the dry leaves. "You staying in or getting out?"

"Staying," I said and told him about Dean, how I just couldn't sit at the cabin anymore, and he offered me a ride.

"We'll go slow and watch for him," he said, and then, "It's a far way in here to spend a winter."

His name was Orrin Wright and he did used to be a cowboy in Nevada, near Utah. His wife died from some horrible kind of cancer, and his daughter did too. So Orrin gave a piece of land to the government to build a ranger station, and the government gave him this job. "Why you both staying so far back in the hills?" he asked.

"The war," I said.

"The war's in Mexico," he said.

"It's here," I said. "It's on the road and in the air. It's on the radio. Everybody in town talks about it. You can't hardly get away from it."

"Not altogether," Orrin said, smiling and showing his horse teeth. "You can't much live on the moon. Or down deep inside the ground. We all got to live where we can see the sky, right here on the skin of the earth. We're connected. The air I breathe out, you breathe in. Right on down the line."

"Me and Dean got no problem living on the earth at all," I said. "It's just there's an awful lot of skin left over where nobody goes and that's where me and Dean go. I can't drink city water. I throw it up before it gets to my stomach. I ain't never been in an elevator. Just the thought of being boxed in with so many people makes my skin itch. I either stay out here or I know I'll shrivel up and die."

Orrin just looked through the windshield, and I knew I shouldn't have said anything about dying because his wife died. Then he said, "You and Dean need to get back up to the cabin before this snow sets in." Already the ground was white, the flakes falling big and heavy, and we weren't even past the big rock yet. I knew what he was thinking about, so I said, "What was your wife's name?"

"Marjorie," he said. And then, "She was my bride. After our honeymoon at the lake, I drove us back through Tonopah and up Railroad Valley. There's a small rough dirt road runs over the hill through the pine nuts to Cherry Creek, and we stopped and got out at the summit. It was just coming June then, and the whole place was covered in lupine, purple and yellow, growed up knee high. The wind was blowing cold and rain moved up the valley like a locomotive, but at the summit the sun came through. I said to Marjorie, 'This is my country.'" That was all he said for a long time, until we reached the highway and started down to town. It was getting dark in the canyon, and there was two inches on the road. That's when my stomach tightened up because I started thinking we wouldn't get back up or maybe I missed Dean, maybe he pulled off the road and we passed him and now he's at the cabin wondering where I am. Maybe I made a big mistake. Every time we saw headlights coming up the canyon, I made Orrin stop and we leaned into the windshield looking for Dean. One time we even blew the horn and flashed the lights, but it wasn't him.

By the time we rolled into town, the cats were crying and it was snowing and blowing like a blizzard. I looked for Dean in every driveway, at the gas station, even the saloon, but it wasn't until we turned into the government building that I saw him driving out. Orrin blocked the road with his truck so Dean had to stop. "You better run," he said, and I did. When I opened the door of the truck and slid across the seat, it was cold as I straddled the shifter and put my arm around Dean. "Long lunch," he said, with his hair going every which way, and I knew he'd been pulling at it. "I waited an hour and a half for them to come back from lunch."

Then Orrin came to Dean's window and asked if we had chains and Dean said, no, but that the old truck was like a sled when the snow got deep and it would go anywhere. But Orrin went to his truck and came back carrying two long tangles of chain that he dropped in the back of our truck. "Bring 'em back in the spring," he said and stepped back into the dark and drove away.

"Are we going to make it to the cabin, Dean?" I asked.

"You bet your ass we'll make it," he said, squinting into the snow. "We're going to stay there, too." The government didn't exactly accept our mining plan, but they didn't flat out reject it either. They needed a little more time, and Dean finally said, "Time's up for today, boys," and that's when I found him.

In the canyon, the snow got deep. There must have been four inches on the road, which meant at least six up above. Then, just like that, one of our headlights burned out. Dean said that's why they build trucks with two lights. We slowed down and when he pushed on the gas again, the back end of the truck came around on the road and Dean turned the wheel so the truck spun around on my side and he turned the wheel again and the truck started moving like a snake up the hill. I knew we needed chains and Dean did too, but it wasn't until it happened again on a curve that we dragged out the rusty chains and stretched them out behind the wheels. Dean backed over the chains and without gloves we hooked them, the snow and frozen chain biting my fingers until I couldn't feel anything. "Let's go," Dean yelled, and I wiped the icy dirt on my dress and climbed in the truck.

Up the canyon we went, chasing that one beam of snow-filled light that could have pulled us into the creek as easy as up the road, one loose link on my side banging against the fender, the whole truck shaking and buzzing like we were driving on a washboard. When we turned off the highway and started up the dirt road, the wind blew hard and the flakes were big and they swirled and made patterns and played tricks on our eyes. I couldn't see anything but the snow and the trees hanging overhead like cobwebs. It was like driving through a tunnel. At the top of the grade where the road dips and switches back by the boulder, Dean slowed. I heard his foot hit the brake, but we kept going. We didn't say a word as the boulder came at us like an iceberg in the fog and we went right into it. Then it was dark outside and quiet, only the black snow hissing against the truck. I was scared for the first time. But the truck started up and Dean got out and came back and told me what I'd already guessed. The headlight was smashed. When we backed up onto the road, Dean gave me the flashlight. "Now lean out the window and shine it back and forth across the road," he said. "Watch for trees."

So that's the way we started, the snow sticking to my eyes and blowing down my neck, the tiny light only a few feet long, filled with white, finding trees almost too late. "To the left," I'd say, and the tree would move off like we were on tracks that brought us close enough to scare us then pulled us away. "To the right, to the right," I'd yell. The road leveled and we passed the Willow Creek bridge, which meant only a mile left. The snow crunched under the wheels, drifting on the dashboard and on the seat, both of us quiet except for my directions. Then the truck bounced and we stopped. Dean pushed on the gas but the truck only rumbled, the chain slapping under the fender with a spray of dirt and rocks.

We got out and shined the light on the rear wheel, half sunk and covered with mud. The snow was almost to my knees. "It's in the creek," Dean said, and he took a long board from the bed. "I'm going to wedge this under here. You drive. When I tell you, put it in second and hit it."

I pushed snow off the seat and got behind the wheel. In the mirror the flashlight flickered and disappeared as Dean worked. I could feel him working. Then I pushed in the clutch and pulled the shifter into second with a slow grinding and I heard Dean call. "Go!" he yelled. And it wasn't until later I found out he yelled, "No!" but I hit it and the truck shook, the speedometer jumped to forty and settled back down. We were still stuck. Looking out the back window I saw the light in the snow, but Dean wasn't there, so I got out and went back, and he was sitting down on the long board. "Lord have mercy," he said as I helped him up and we got back into the truck and tried again. The wheels whistled and dug deeper. Dean said, "Let's go home." So we started walking, him holding me under the arm with one hand and holding the flashlight in the other, through the knee-deep snow. The cats kept crying in the basket, and the snow melted in my boots, blowing into my eyes like sand.

We didn't talk while we walked. There was nothing to say. I thought about frostbite, but I didn't say it because I didn't want to scare Dean. We just thought about lifting our legs over the snow, coming down and pushing forward and then one time the wind came across my face and I smelled woodsmoke. I couldn't feel my feet and I was afraid, and then I smelled it again. "We're home," Dean said.

"Sweet home," I said.

Against the snow we pulled the screen door open and went into the cabin. It was quiet inside and still warm. Both of us kneeling in front of the stove, we took turns blowing on the coals, feeling the heat on our faces as Dean added wood and it swelled into flame. We changed our clothes and hung the wet ones over the stove. Then we laid on the bed, listening to the fire and to the snow against the window as the cats rolled on the floor and the lamplight made their shadows big on the wall. For a few minutes, we turned on the radio and they said it was snowing two inches an hour and by tomorrow Carson City would have two feet, which meant we'd have four.

I thought about Orrin Wright, what he told me about not being able to live on the moon. In my mind I left the warm orange light of the cabin and rose into the storm, looking down from the top of the red fir. I could see dim light in the windows and the smoke that mixed with snow, falling through the trees, washing over the crest. The big flakes swirled around me, played tricks on my eyes as I knew I was rising over the pines, over the peaks until the snowflakes turned to stars. As far as I could see, the earth curved away like a lens and I started falling, slowly, into the clouds and into the snow and the warm light of the cabin. I watched Dean sleep and wondered what he was dreaming. When I kissed his forehead he opened his eyes and said, "We're home," and he closed his eyes and fell asleep. Then I put my head on his chest and slept too.

In the morning, the sun came through the curtains. I pulled them back and saw long windy clouds blowing over the cabin and over the old volcano. When I tried to open the screen door, the snow was too deep, but I pushed it and packed it back enough to squeeze through. Snow fell from the pines, drifting against my face as I pushed through the deep snow. I turned back toward the cabin and saw Dean in the window waving. I put my hands on my head and lifted my face into the wind. From the chimney, new smoke started, which meant Dean was feeding the fire, so I moved up to the mine and searched for the pick handle, but it was buried. With my arms I skimmed through the snow until I hit it. I pushed the snow away, digging down until I had a place to stand, and I piled it up with my hands. Dean came out of the cabin and pulled snow off the woodpile and carried a load back inside. He saw me in the mine and told me the coffee was cooking.

Right to the ground I cleared the pit and looked at the spot where the steel pick touched the earth. I imagined that it had sent down a thick taproot deep into the ground. I shook the pick and it twisted, moving in its hole until it let go and I held it over my head and brought it down again. With my gloves I scooped some dirt together and cupped it in my hands before casting it out like seed over the new snow.

I pictured the heavy roots of the red fir stretching into the ground, deep below the snow where the wind did not blow and it was still warm. The squirrels curled up in their round burrows, waiting for spring. I felt the snow melting already, seeping between the rocks, softening my skin that winter until the dirt I had thrown over the snow settled down to rest on the earth again.

WILD

COW

We rode in the dark, the two of us, under the stars. After a whole day of tracking, we hadn't caught sight of her, but we trailed her over the summit to Quinn Canyon. I couldn't see my father, but I could hear his horse crunching over the sagebrush next to me and I could hear him talk. "I never seen her up close," he said, "but she's big and long-horned." I couldn't see my own horse right under me, but I could feel her falter, picking her steps carefully through the washes, and I could see the stars. They were sharp because it was very cold, and my toes went numb in my boots as we crossed the belly of the big valley. I was lost. My father must have been following the stars, but they all looked the same to me and my feet were frozen and I couldn't imagine the cabin was so far off.

"I'd rather be too hot than too cold," I said. "I can take the heat."

"You ever been thirsty?" He sounded annoyed, like I'd said something without thinking it all the way through.

"I been thirsty."

"I mean *real* thirsty," he said. "Craving for water drives a person crazy. The cold takes you over slow and easy, like going to sleep."

"Never been *that* thirsty."

He made his point that night with every star in the sky as witness. And he'd done it before, but never in a mean-spirited way, showing me that I didn't know everything there was to know simply because I'd been to college. On the day I left for school, he looked down at me from his favorite horse, his eyes shaded by the brim of his old Western hat, and said, "I hope you learned somethin' while you were here." I told him I did. I thought I had learned about honesty and fairness and the payoff for a hard day's work. But since the whole affair has settled firmly in my memory like layers of mud and dust, I know I didn't learn shit about that. I learned to have a healthy respect for a wild cow. Plain and simple. A wild cow is a dangerous thing.

By the time we got to the cabin, a little moon had come over the mountains and we could see enough to unsaddle the horses and toss a few flakes of hay into the corral. My feet were so numb it felt like I was walking on my knees and my nose was running and I was hungry. Inside the cabin, he lit the kerosene lamps while I cut kindling on the big stone hearth and the feeling came back slowly to my feet.

"A wild cow in the hills don't wanna be caught," he said. He'd seen her a couple of times, by chance, in the high country. Like a mountain lion, she never came down into the wide-open valley. She probably didn't even see herself as a cow, or recognize the other cattle as members of her own kind. She belonged to the family Bovidae, hoofed and hollow-horned. She was a Hereford. Born in the hills, she was destined for the stockyards, for dinner plates, to be someday served up as top sirloin or rump roast like the rest. But she'd avoided all that.

"She's long-horned," he said as we warmed our hands

over the cookstove. "And wild-horned." From what he'd seen, her horns were more than two feet long and sharp as daggers. And she was big—easily over a ton, he figured. But while one of her horns curved up in the normal way, the other one hooked forward like a lance.

She had no brand. No one really *owned* her. But the Forest Service had told us to get her off the hill because she lived on land we leased each year. They knew she was there, saw her big tracks in the snow, and things were just starting to get bad between the government and the cowboys in those days. They said that cattle overgraze the wild feed meant for the *real* wild animals like deer and antelope, that their heavy hooves tromp wildflowers and tender vegetation and their massive cow pies spoil the meadows and creeks.

"They used us," my father said, prying open a heavy can of hash. "They ran the Indians out with the cavalry and set us up to hold the place with our cattle, and now they don't need us no more. They told me people won't be eatin' so much beef on account of the colostrum."

"Cholesterol."

"Cholesterol," he repeated, setting it in his memory.

"We could raise ostriches," I said.

"No ostriches. I ain't a bird farmer."

"It's a thing of the future," I told him. "The big outfits in Texas raise ostriches. They're a little expensive at first, but once you get goin' they pay off. The eggs go for a thousand dollars each. You sell the feathers. And the hide is real soft and tougher than a cow's. The whole bird ain't nothing more than a few hundred pounds of walkin' breast meat. It's all dark meat and *looks* like beef, so people can take to it real easy, but it's low in fat and cholesterol. *And,* you raise them in pens, so you don't have to chase 'em all over the mountain."

"Wouldn't know how to rope one," he said.

"That's just bein' stubborn."

He looked at me with his lips pursed, like his face was made of stone.

"Cows," he said, "is all I know."

At dawn we saddled the horses and moved out along the two-track road by the creek with our hands in our pockets and the reins held against our bodies, the horses following the road as they naturally do.

"All this over one cow," I said. We stopped and looked back over the valley toward Water Gap and Mail Summit, over the long, soundless succession of mountain and valley and mountain. I didn't want to be there, searching the frozen hills for a single, silly cow. I had better things to do, but the old man was on a mission and I had no choice but to follow him. We moved out, winding through the sage, cutting through the willow and the wild rose along the creek and climbing slowly toward the summit.

By midmorning, it had warmed. When we reached Cherry Creek summit and started down the rocky and difficult ground to Quinn Canyon, we picked up her tracks in the snow. She had come there early that morning, meandering, pushing at the new snow with her broad nose. With her tongue, she had found the tender stalks of ricegrass between the rocks and rabbit brush. Her tracks were old and windblown, still wandering and unaware of us. But as our horses sidestepped across a slope of loose rock, her tracks became crisper, more direct, cutting straight between one point and the next, picking the most difficult path as if she knew she was being trailed.

Through the junipers we followed her, into the piñon pine, the lower dead branches scraping us as we ducked and weaved between them. Snow fell down our necks from the trees. Up on a side hill, we followed her, where her tracks widened and deepened in the loose dirt.

"She's running," my father said.

"She knows we're here," I said.

"She knew that an hour ago," he said.

But when we dropped back down around the creek, we lost her. Her tracks went into the water but didn't come out. I looked along the opposite bank, the red hips of wild rose and wild currant still holding snow, but no sign of a wild cow.

"She's followin' the creek," he said. "Stayin' in the water."

We picked our way downstream for five minutes before I saw where she had climbed out and headed straight uphill. My father laughed. "Dirty pot licker!" He knew what she had done before I did. When we broke through the trees, into a clearing of rock and sage, I recognized the dirt road that crossed the summit to Cherry Creek and realized we'd been fooled.

"She took us in a loop, but now she's scared. Now she's movin' out." He pointed to a cow pie. It was a fresh one, long and trailing, dropped on the run. By noon the snow had melted everywhere except in the shade, but the ground was soft and moist and we tracked her back down, pushing the horses through clearings, cantering when we could. We rode down Scofield Canyon and picked up the Goat Ranch road, and the horses were tired and lathered by the time we reached the meadow at Quinn Canyon.

The meadow is a small place with a long history going back to Willis Welsh and then to Indian times as far back as anybody cares. Willis came from Scotland to run cattle back in the twenties, and my father told how one day Willis went to Tempiute by horse cart, a trip that took a full day. It was winter and he left his wife at the cabin. On the way back from the spring with a bucket of water, she slipped on the ice and broke her leg and died from exposure. Willis found her when he got back. It broke his spirit. He packed up and moved to California.

The meadow was also the site of the last Indian massacre by the cavalry. My father told that Verne Newman, an old cowboy who lives alone near Water Gap, found cavalry buttons around the meadow, brass buttons with "U.S." on them. He also found baskets in small caves where the Indians stashed their babies when they heard the soldiers coming.

These stories are true. The stone chimney of Willis Welsh's cabin still stands right in the middle of the meadow, along with a few withered posts from his old corral. And at the far end of the meadow, you can still see two rock walls stretching like a large V through the sagebrush, where the Indians chased game into a box canyon for the kill.

By the time we reached the meadow, my knees were sore from five hours of riding in the cold. I could hardly walk. We tied the horses and I hobbled out into the meadow, trying to get my knees working again, stomping the cold out of my feet. When I turned back, my father was standing like a deer and pointing with his thumb.

"There she is," he whispered.

I couldn't see her. But then she moved and I spotted her big flank between the cedar trees. She looked like a rhinoceros, roan-colored and muscular, lean for that time of year. Moving smoothly on the rim of the meadow, she turned her head in my direction and I saw the horns, just like my father had said, one up and one down, as she broke into a full run and charged me.

She had her head down and her eyes were on me and that long forward horn was coming for me. I tried to run, but my knees locked and I hobbled as fast as I could. I heard her hooves pounding and I heard her breathing like a locomotive. With her nose, she touched the back of my leg. Then she got under my butt with her nose again and lifted me right off the ground, running me to the edge of the meadow in midair, flicking me up like a flake of hay.

I fell on my belly in the sagebrush, and the cow tripped over me and fell on top of me. I remember the cracking sound, but I didn't think it was my ribs. I jumped up and the cow jumped up and she ran away up the rocks. My father asked me if I was all right. I told him I was. I thought I'd simply gotten the wind knocked out of me. So I climbed up on Molly and we were off, right on her tail, running through the sage, heading for the trees.

We came up behind her, and she bawled like cows do when they're scared and ran in a straight line without even trying to shake us off. As we cleared the meadow and climbed, I felt the pain in my back like a knife and I slouched over and grabbed the saddle horn with one hand to keep from bouncing. My father saw me and I could see his lips saying, "You all right?" and I shook my head no, but we kept going, as he already had a large loop of rope sailing over his head. His first shot fell short, landed on the cow's back and slipped off to the side.

"Cut 'er off," he yelled. "Don't let 'er down the hill."

It was a steep hill, covered with loose, flat rock and small, scruffy trees—not a place to be running a horse. But I remember the look on my father's face, the one he gets when he makes up his mind to do something. His face seems to be made of stone. He sat back in his saddle, the loop of rope idling again over his head as I tried to get the cow turned around, but I wasn't fast enough.

The big critter had built up a head of steam as she hit the lip of that hill. Just as she thought she was home free, my father threw the rope and it landed loosely around her head. When he pulled up the slack, the cow tried to shake it off and the rope cinched up solid around her horns. He made his dallies, wrapping the rope quickly around the saddle horn and holding it there with one hand. The other hand pulled the reins on Jim, the biggest, stoutest, most sure-footed horse I ever knew, trying to slow him down, but the cow was big and stout and surefooted, too.

Over the hill went the cow and over the hill went my father, the rope between them stretched tight. The cow was scared and Jim was scared, but my father stayed in the saddle and moved with the horse like he was glued to it. He made it look effortless, which it wasn't, his face expressionless except for his eyes, which narrowed and watched every move the wild cow made.

Down the hill they went, my father pulling up the reins and Jim sitting back, trying to dig in his hind hooves, but the ground kept giving way and he backpedaled and skidded down the slope. Then I heard a noise like an old tree splitting in half and I wouldn't have believed it if I hadn't seen it with my own eyes, but the whole front half of my father's saddle ripped right out from under him. The whole pommel came off, but he held on to the rope and it zipped through his hand before he even knew what happened. The cow did a somersault over the rocks, came back up on her feet and kept going downhill, dragging the rope and the pommel of the saddle through the trees.

My father looked down between his legs. He puckered his lips and looked over at me and appeared to be whistling, but no sound came out. We watched the wild cow barreling away. And when the pommel got caught in the crotch of a cedar, we heard the rope snap like the crack of a whip without slowing the cow down a bit. That was the last time we ever saw the wild cow, but we still think about her from time to time.

We rode to where the chunk of saddle had wedged in the tree. When my father picked it up, I saw that his right hand was bleeding where the rope had burned through.

"She's bigger than the both of us." He pressed his hand against the leg of his jeans.

"We could come back and shoot her," I said.

"Some things are better left alone."

My bones were cold and I was hungry and my knees hurt and I knew my ribs were broken because every time I moved or took a deep breath, it felt like a knife blade in my back. My father didn't complain, never did in the thirty-three years I knew him. From time to time, he looked at the palm of his hand and I could see the flesh was ripped clean off. He hung on to that wild cow right up to the last inch.

"Looks like it hurts," I said.

"Hurts deep," he said, and I figured he wasn't talking about his hand.

"We'll come back," I said.

"Nope."

And somewhere in Quinn Canyon the wild cow slept that night, as we showered and mended our bodies as best we could, as we blessed our meal and shared the story of our defeat. Sure as anything, the big cow hunkered down in the sagebrush or in the willows with a short piece of rope still hanging from her horns. She listened carefully to the sounds around her, the normal sounds of the night she knew so well, and she thought back on what had happened that day, if cows can do that. She learned the limits of what humans will do for no good reason. She learned more, as we had, about the real meaning of endurance and stamina. She felt the burning in her lungs, starving for air. In a short time, the piece of rope would slip from her horns when she dipped her head to drink from a creek and she would not notice it drifting downstream, turning with the current and slowly sinking. Before long, there would be no trace of our encounter, no monument in stone, no record of our tiresome ride.

For a week we rested. I had broken three ribs and cracked

one, way around where they connect to the backbone. My father's hand kept oozing and cracking every time he moved it. Although he hung the pommel of his torn saddle on the wall of the shop like a trophy, he didn't talk about the wild cow, but I could tell that he still thought about her sometimes as he sat and stared at the palm of his hand.

After church on Sunday, I saw him standing in the alfalfa by himself and figured something was up. I walked over the ditch and across the field.

"They're gonna be *your* birds," he said.

He paced a line parallel to the ditch and dug a furrow with the heel of his boot. Checking his angles, he paced evenly across the low alfalfa, stopping again to mark the field with his boot before turning and pacing and marking the third corner and coming back to where I was standing.

We worked together and drove all the way to Cedar City with the horse trailer to get pipe and chain-link fabric and I never asked him *why* he changed his mind, although I guess I knew. It must have been old age that softened him, as it slowly softens even the toughest cowboys. He'd spent his entire life fighting the cold and the heat, the tendency of machines to break and of water to flow where it will. And he did it always without the appearance of a struggle. He made it look easy. But even broncobusters and bull riders get old someday and begin to falter, as my father did.

About two weeks later, just before dawn, we heard a ruckus in the ostrich pen. The birds were high-stepping and twirling, fanning their wings and hissing like they do when they're angry, and we saw a coyote running across the alfalfa, heading for the hills. One of the fence posts was bent outward and the chain-link fabric was bowed as if a truck had run into it. We'd had no idea they were so powerful. My father lifted a handful of fresh alfalfa, and the largest ostrich, Rosco was his name, arched his neck over the fence and started pecking at the little brass button on the cuff of my father's denim jacket.

"Look at him," he said. "Just peckin' away at that button like it was somethin' real special."

He stood there with his arm in the air as Rosco focused on the brass button and stabbed at it with his beak. He pecked and pulled without stopping and my father kept his arm up and watched the bird with pure and simple pride, a tall, lean old man, breathing easily and lightly. As the sun came over the hills, I felt the warmth on my face, and the frost on the alfalfa turned to steam all around us. I remembered the night we rode through the valley in the cold, how I depended on him for direction to the cabin.

"You were right," I said. "I *would* rather be too cold than too hot."

He smiled as if he was surprised that I remembered what he'd told me.

A month later, I visited Verne Newman, who lived alone in a small cabin near Water Gap. He told me he was born in the same cabin—showed me the very spot, made me touch it with my hand—and assured me he'd die there too. When I told him the story of the wild cow, he smiled and looked at me with watery blue eyes like he'd heard it all before. He showed me the old basket he'd found in a small cave above the meadow, a basket that still held the feathery bones of an Indian baby. Then he shuffled across the wooden floor, reached up on a shelf and came back with a baby-food jar. He shook the jar gently until several buttons rolled into the palm of his hand, brass buttons with "U.S." on them. With his thumb, he turned them over slowly and told me about the day he'd found them in the meadow. He spoke softly, reverently, like old men sometimes do, and only a handful of people have heard this story.

TEACHER'S PAY

My father drove to Reno last month and the trouble started all over again like it does every time he shows up. As usual, I put my drum in the garage. It's not that he'd be upset or disappointed by my drumming. He simply would not understand, just as he cannot understand why we have no children. "Having a family," he says, "ain't something you think too much about. It just happens." But he never had to understand the *science* of it all, never had to imagine the frantic path of sperm or the orbit of a single egg. I could never explain to him how hard we're trying. And I couldn't explain *why* I drum, the unbearable pressure I feel to be a father, which I can't even explain to myself. The drumming lets me forget.

My old man, gray haired but tough as a badger, was a cowboy to the last drop, dressed in denim and a Western hat and boots as he backed up our driveway behind the wheel of his big Oldsmobile. He stood on the porch, legs a little bowed from riding horses since he was a boy, holding a small leather suitcase in one hand and a cooler in the other. When he saw us, he took off his hat, something he rarely does.

Above the brim line, his forehead was pure white and the rest of his face was the color of cowhide, his thin lips seemingly sewn on with tight stitches. He held up the cooler and smiled from the corners of his mouth, and I knew it meant trouble.

"Calf fries," Bonnie whispered, not because it was any secret. The words simply slipped out with her breath. She knew he was never going to give up trying to get me to eat those things.

"Fresh." My father smiled like a frog. He set the cooler on the table and lifted out a plastic container, which he held with both hands, carefully swirling the contents, feeling the weight.

"Kinda high in cholesterol, aren't they, honey?" Bonnie asked me.

"Kinda."

My father waited for Bonnie to move out of earshot.

"Fries," he said, "put lead in your pencil."

I didn't need lead in my pencil. I didn't need it then and I didn't need it the first time he'd said it to me, when I was seventeen and had more lead in my pencil than I knew what to do with. We lived in Adaven—which is "Nevada" spelled backward—forty miles down a dirt road on the lip of a long valley in the absolute middle of nowhere. No gangs, no drugs, no violence. No movies, no restaurants, and no girls. Only cows and sagebrush and all the fresh air I could handle, and then some.

It was cutting and branding time and it was cold. It was the coldest December I'd ever seen, and we worked hard all day, the three of us—my father and me and Uncle Jay. I stood by the branding fire, a fifty-gallon drum with a hole in the side, warming my hands, feeding it sticks of cedar and sagebrush, keeping the irons hot. My uncle Jay roped a calf and dragged it into position.

First I flipped him and my father moved in. From the fire I took an iron, the embers clinging to it, shining like diamonds in the cold wind and crackling as I put my foot down on his flank. When I pushed the iron against him, he bellowed like a siren and his eyes bugged out and his tongue stuck straight out like the stamen in a wildflower, but he didn't move. I rocked the iron against his hide, rolling the hot steel back and forth so it didn't stick, searing the skin, burning an even brand.

I took off my gloves and opened my pocketknife. It was a small knife, but very sharp. With one hand I grabbed the calf's sac, pulling it tight and sawcutting with my knife. His blood was warm and felt good on my fingers because the wind was so cold. I searched for the testicles he had unknowingly drawn up away from danger, milking them down through the opening I'd made. Like a couple of plums, I held them in the palm of my hand, the two cords running between my fingers to someplace deep in his innards. I pulled them tight and ran my knife back and forth along the length of the cords and gave them to my father.

I had just enough time to wipe my hands on my jeans and wipe my knife and pull on my gloves. And that's the way the whole day went—flip and stick and slit—until the sun touched the mountains west of us and we were done. The cattle were quiet. The branding fire had died. It was cold and I was hungry and we leaned against the corral, the three of us, and rested.

"Job's done," my father said, kicking at something in the dirt.

"Worked up a large hunger," Uncle Jay said.

They dragged their boots through the loose dirt, churning up things that were better left buried until they turned up the bundles of baling wire they were looking for. My father handed me a piece of rusty wire, which I took without looking at him. From the cedar rail, they selected their testicles and carefully wrapped them with wire, holding them over the embers of the branding fire in the fifty-gallon drum.

"Puts lead in your pencil," my father told me. That was the first time he said it.

And there, in the old corral halfway between nowhere and no place, with no witness but the wind and a herd of weary cattle, I leaned back and dreamed of a different life for myself. I didn't want to be a cowboy. I wanted to go to college and be a teacher, which I did, so I wouldn't have to work outside in the rain and the cold and the stinking heat of summer. I didn't want to bust my back, which had already given signs of an early failure. And I didn't care about cows, or their manure.

My father and his brother stood by the fire, dressed in leather and denim, and held the calf fries lightly between their fingers, looking at each other and smiling like frogs because they had done this before and they knew they would do it again. But I refused. I didn't want to be a cowboy for the rest of my life. And just the *smell* of those things gave me the chills.

"Yes sir!" my father said. And then to me he said, "Jason, you gotta stop thinking so hard about it and put one down the pipe. The fun's in the tryin' of it."

"I can't."

I couldn't. As if the simple ceremony in the bottom of that big valley would've locked me into a lifetime of baling hay and tending cows and hauling their manure. I didn't join them as they had once joined their father and he had probably joined his, so on and so forth all the way back to the days of the first castration. Before that, there was something else, I'm sure, that signified what a man is supposed to do, bringing father and son together with something more than a common name. But I refused. "I can't," I'd said. And I didn't.

We closed the corral and climbed onto our horses and started across the valley toward home. I rode out ahead. "You just gotta stop thinking so hard about it," my father had said, but I couldn't. I thought about it as I squeezed my heels against Jolina's flank and she moved out through a sandy wash. I kept thinking about it when I wrapped my legs tightly against her and kicked her once as she galloped over the low sage. I kicked her again and stretched forward into the wind, listening to her measured breath, closing my eyes and feeling the pounding of her hooves in the dirt, leaving the two men far behind. I still think about it today.

Bonnie came into the kitchen rolling her eyes and flopping her arms as if she was going to fly right out of the room.

"He's at it again," she said. "Hasn't been here an hour and he's already beating around the bush about babies!"

"He's an old man," I said. "He's leaving tomorrow."

"You gotta tell him we're doing everything we can. I don't know which way is up anymore."

"He doesn't realize."

I opened my arms and hugged her. She pressed her head against my chest. I smelled her hair and kissed her neck and we danced slowly on the kitchen floor until we simply stood there holding each other without moving and without speaking.

A few minutes later, my father came out of the shower wearing clean jeans and a long-sleeve shirt, his thin hair slicked back wet. From the refrigerator he pulled the plastic container of calf fries and set to work on the counter.

"Butterflied, breaded, and barbecued," he said. "The best."

We ate on the picnic table under the lilac. It was 103 degrees in the shade and it wasn't fifteen minutes into the meal before he mentioned something about being a grandfather and Bonnie looked at me like she wanted me to tell him the whole story, but I didn't. I couldn't tell him about the countless sperm tests and egg tests, the temperature taking, tube cleaning, zinc pills, daily hormone injections all up and down Bonnie's long legs, the poking and prodding and sticking and peeping, all of which had already flatly failed. Instead, I changed the subject.

Bonnie glared at me over a forkful of chicken. I simply couldn't do it. He wouldn't understand, not an old man who had sprung from a farm like wild asparagus, where cows and horses and cats and dogs popped up like weeds, arrived as easily as the wind. To him, they were simply something that *happened,* like rain or manure, not something you think too much about. And that's exactly what he'd say: "You just gotta stop thinking so hard about it."

After lunch, we sat back on lawn chairs in the sun, my father and me. Over a hundred degrees and he sat there in jeans and a long-sleeve shirt and boots. I never in my life saw him in shorts, or even in a short-sleeve shirt. He never wore sunglasses. He looked as out of place on a lawn chair in our suburban backyard as a big-screen TV in a log cabin. He was an old man, an old-time cowboy who had barely learned to read and write, who had worked bone hard since he was a boy, every day except Sunday. When he dies, I'm sure it will be in the course of some job, while sitting on a horse or on a tractor. But for the time being, he simply looked fidgety on the lawn chair, restless under the surface.

"Y'know," he said, looking at his hands in his lap, "maybe it was *how* we cooked them calf fries that bothered you." He groaned and sat up in the chair so the sun hit him full in the face.

"That was twenty years ago," I said. "It doesn't matter."

"Maybe your taste buds've changed."

"Could have," I said. "My forehead's higher. And my belly button's deeper."

He laughed. He always thought I had a good sense of humor. And maybe it was the angle of the sun that day, or the temperature, or the combination of a number of things that revealed deep cracks in the leather of his face, the yellow and brown in his eyes, his worn teeth, cupped and tarnished like the teeth of an old horse, his tired chin. For the first time, I caught a glimpse of what I would someday become and figured maybe I'd missed a chance back in that cold and windy valley in the middle of nowhere, not something that would've made any big difference in my life, but something that had followed me nonetheless and had become as much a part of who I am as my posture or my fingerprints or the belly button I was born with.

He looked at me, his eyes shaded by the brim of his Western hat and said, "If I cook 'em good, here on the grill with barbecue sauce till they're done well and just crispy, would you try one?"

What else could I say? He took me by surprise. My old man, closer to death's doorstep than most folks on earth, and he asks me to simply *try* something. Just for him. While he's a guest in my house. I said the only thing I could say.

"Sure."

He sprang from his chair like a puppy and came back with the tongs and a plate of calf fries piled up like a pyramid. Through a pool of barbecue sauce, he dredged them and set them carefully on the grill. When they were done, Bonnie came back with the camera and sized us up in the viewfinder.

"Go for it, you ramblin' buckaroos," she said. "Move closer together."

We stood shoulder to shoulder, my father in boots and jeans and Western hat and me in shorts and a T-shirt and flip-flops. He handed me a fry and took one for himself, holding it precisely between his thumb and first finger, both of us standing there with our fingers spread as if signaling that everything was A-OK. Bonnie clicked the picture as we chewed. It's like chicken liver, I thought. Like an oyster. But I knew it wasn't. My father ate another one, a small one, in one bite.

"C'mon," he said. "Dig in."

"Nope."

And that was it. He ate a few more and Bonnie wrapped the rest in plastic. The next morning he left, rolling slowly down our driveway in his highly chromed Oldsmobile with tinted windows, air-conditioning, and the paper plate of calf fries on the seat next to him. It's a five-hour drive from Reno to Hiko, clear across Nevada, and I knew the plate would be empty by the time he hit Tonopah. As he swung into the street, Bonnie and I stood on the sidewalk and waved, but he didn't see us. With both big hands on the wheel, he was busy watching the road, driving cautiously because he was in a big city. But he'd be fine once he got past Fallon and the road stretched out long into the valleys. Besides, he'd already said good-bye. That's just the way he was, not too many wasted motions. I figured he was already thinking about the ranch, about feeding or irrigating or fixing a gate. We'd see him again on Thanksgiving.

When we went back in the house, Bonnie lay on her back on the living room rug with her hands behind her head.

"It's ours again," she said, smiling. "I feel like we've gotten our house back again." She looked at me seriously. "Is that bad?"

"No," I said. "It's good."

I knelt next to her and put my hands on her thighs and squeezed her just above the knees because I knew this was her most ticklish spot. She threw her legs around me, catching me around the waist, and we rolled over on the rug. I tried to grab her hands, but she kept breaking free and tickling my sides and the only way I could stop her was by squeezing her thighs. "Stop," she'd yell and just when I'd let up, she went after me again. Wc laughed and screamed and pushed the coffee table across the floor until we were out of breath and my muscles were tired and she kissed me quickly and the wrestling became serious and we pulled off our clothes. We did it right there on the living room rug for the first time. Then we went to our bedroom and drew the blinds and made long and sweetly satisfying love again.

The next day was Monday, and that night I drummed. When I turned the key in my truck, it sputtered and popped and barely started. It's an old Nissan that I nurse along with chewing gum and baling wire. It has over three hundred thousand miles on it, but I can't afford to buy a new one now, not on teacher's pay, not with a baby maybe on the way.

In the church hall, I carried my drum to my usual seat by the stage. Henry starts us off, as usual, twirling his mallets to get our attention, and then *boom* and *boomboom.* He lets the vibration fill the room before damping it down and we listen as he rolls a low wave of thunder that builds and falls and builds higher until we're off, slowly at first.

I close my eyes, like I always do, and wrap my legs around the curve of my drum. First I nod my head, rapping out the rolling beat of a horse's hooves pounding through dirt, feeling them all the way up through my seat as we loosen and stretch into the long valley. The ground is flat as glass, nothing to hit even if we try. I tap my foot to the rhythm of our stride until I can hear the wind in my ears and feel the warmth of the sun on my face as we run randomly over the low sage. *You just gotta stop thinking so hard about it,* I whisper, *relax,* but the words are blown back by the wind. I squeeze in my heels and stretch forward so we pick up speed and the steady beat of hooves becomes a drumroll, a diesel engine breathing and pushing me like a locomotive across the valley as we go and go. I close my eyes and feel the tears the wind has made.

But in time my horse tires and we sink back to an easy rhythm of running and breathing, my eyes wide open and wondering *where* and *why.* My muscles relax and I feel like I know where I have come from and where I am heading and for a moment I can smell only the sweetness of my horse and the strong smell of sage. I slouch in my seat, loosen my legs and listen to the drumming. Like thunder it rolls along the walls of our room as Henry smiles, his head cocked like a robin listening for worms, until only he continues playing quietly, rumbling and damping and rumbling again, and it's over.

By the time I left, it was already dark and I got the usual popping and cranking and near starting I had grown used to when I turned the key in my truck. It had two bald tires, a wild crack in the windshield that looked like a tumbleweed, faded paint and body rot here and there from road salt. An old piece of rug covered a small hole in the floor and kept the exhaust gases out, but it got me around and that's all I really cared about. Once it got going, it ran like a wild horse.

As I cruised across town, I felt somehow satisfied with myself for the time I'd just spent and for the small tribute I'd paid my father the previous day. It wasn't a conscious decision to make him happy and it wasn't an accident either. It simply *happened,* at a good time, for whatever reasons, or simply for no reason at all. I put my elbow out the window on Main Street, sailing home on a tailwind, making all the green lights, feeling like anything was possible. I waved to an old man walking alone by a dark building, and he waved back as if we were old friends.

When the garage door finally came down behind me, I sat in the dark for a long time, thinking about my good fortune, about the countless second and third chances that life so generously offers as it pours over me like an endless gift. "The fun's in the trying," my father had said. He never gave advice, only hoped I'd learn something along the way, nodding like he already knew I'd someday find words for the stories of everything that has ever happened, or ever will. I sat there breathing easily and lightly until Bonnie finally opened the door. She stood in the backlight of the kitchen, smiling, arms open, wearing the blue satin nightgown that I love, her light hair tousled, and reminded me that it was finally time for bed.

HEADING FOR THE HOLY LAND

Elias Mose leaned into a cold wind blowing flat across the edge of Nevada, standing like a statue outside the Butane Cafe, dressed in the remnants of two blue suits. As if posing for a picture, he kept one hand on a shopping cart full of his things, neatly packed into every square inch and wrapped in plastic for protection against dust and rain. The cart looked out of place because the truck stop was ninety miles from the nearest real supermarket, plunked down in the middle of nowhere at the confluence of two roads that shimmered off like ancient rivers into the sagebrush. It was just December, the whole country poised on the lip of winter, holding its breath before the final and fast tumble into darkness.

From the west, Murray Stichell rolled into the parking lot, driving his old truck with no door on the driver's side, the heater blowing hot air over his shoulder and straight into the high desert sky. He didn't see Elias Mose at first because he was busy searching for the white Jeep his wife, Valerie, had been driving, rubbing his thighs with both hands and thinking. Murray had lost his wife again.

He didn't really *lose* her like he would lose a cow in the

hills or the keys to his truck. He knew where she was. He just couldn't get to her, going on six hours now, with dinnertime come and gone and a blood-red sun resting on the western hills. It was the third time she simply hadn't shown up like this, and each time she'd been with Miriam Higby, wife of Verne Higby, the ostrich farmer.

Twice already, she'd stayed out all night listening to coyotes yammering above Cherry Creek summit, watching clouds race like wild horses in front of the moon. That's what she told Murray. Cherry Creek was a place Murray could not get to because he had a bad foot and hated horses. Both times, he sat home and waited. Every rush of wind or chuckle from the creek brought him to the window, but he only saw the quiet face of the mountain. When Valerie finally showed up, she didn't talk too much about it. "I needed a little time by myself," she'd said, bleary-eyed from a whole night under the stars. "Some wide-open space." A few days later it was all forgotten, until it happened again.

Without saying a word, Elias Mose grabbed his spray bottle and a crumpled ball of newspaper and descended upon Murray's windshield like a hungry bird, spraying and rubbing and spraying, smearing the dirt in circles. Murray just sat there. Because it was cold, the water started to freeze in fan-shaped crystals, but Elias Mose worked faster and harder until the glass came clear. He stepped back and smiled.

"I guess you need travelin' money," Murray said. Having spent most of his fifty-three years judging animals by the little movements they made, he'd developed an eye for people too.

"I'm going to Jerusalem," Elias Mose said.

Murray scratched the back of his hand. He figured Elias Mose was thinking of Jerusalem, Texas, the home of Power Choice Tractors, or Jerusalem, Montana, where his cousin lived, or some other little town called Jerusalem for no real reason right here in the United States.

"Texas?" Murray said, it being too cold for Montana.

"Jerusalem." Elias Mose put his hands together in front of his heart. "The Holy Land."

Murray lived in Adaven, a twisted ribbon of green meadow tucked in the foothills of a mountain range in the middle of nowhere. Although he was a Mormon, he was not a traveling man. He'd never even *been* to Texas or Montana. He'd never been farther from home than Salt Lake City, once, but he knew darn well there was no way to roll a shopping cart all the way to the Holy Land. He scratched his forehead with his knuckles and watched Elias Mose with the same careful eye he used to size up a wild cow, scrutinizing every shift of his fingers, the measure of his breathing.

"Help me find my wife and I'll pay you twenty dollars," he said.

"You lost her?" Elias Mose pulled on his black beard with both hands.

"I know where she is," Murray said, "but I can't get there with this bad foot."

Elias Mose looked down and saw that Murray's left boot was curled up at the toe like a leprechaun's shoe. He felt sorry for the cowboy and he needed the money, so they shook hands and hoisted the shopping cart into the back of the truck, which was jumbled with engine parts and toolboxes and pieces of junk.

Cherry Creek summit was a wild place, reachable only on foot or on horseback, but Murray didn't get along with horses. He distrusted them because they were so unpredictable. He did much better with machinery, pistons and levers and gears he could take apart and put back together so he knew exactly what was going on inside.

The last time Murray rode a horse, he was twenty-three

and newly married to Valerie. He was out pheasant hunting when his horse suddenly reared up and went right over backward on top of him, which would've been all right except his shotgun fired and blew his foot off, boot and all. He didn't shoot his *whole* foot off, just all the toes and most of the arch, leaving the heel and some of the side part.

By the time Murray and Elias Mose reached the Cherry Creek turnoff, it was almost dark. A sheet of silver clouds had risen like a crown over the western hills, illuminated by a big, grinning moon. The sky shimmered like deep and uncertain water when the first few stars appeared, wavering, as if slowly rising to the surface. They snaked along the edge of a deep wash, rising out of the valley bottom. Every now and then, a small juniper appeared out of the darkness, standing above the sagebrush like a pale ghost in the moonlight. The road was rough and Murray's headlights were dim and Elias Mose felt as if they were driving through a tunnel with no end. High above them, the mountain peaks pushed into the sky, nameless and looming.

As they entered the forest, Elias Mose told Murray about a woman he'd met in Las Vegas just a few days earlier.

"She was a wild one," he said. "Crazy lady from the mountains come into town for the weekend. Smelled like woodsmoke and diesel fuel, and her hands were rough and dirty."

Murray admitted he'd never had such an experience, having been with only one woman in his life. Then he told Elias Mose something he'd never told anyone before, because there's something about driving in the wilderness in the pitch of night that brings out hidden truths in men. Stories float to the surface, dislodged from the rocky places where they've been wedged, for years sometimes, to find air again. Murray told Elias Mose that in twenty years of marriage, he and Valerie had never seen each other naked.

"You're shittin' me," Elias Mose said.

"I ain't," Murray assured him.

"No wonder she's up there hootin' at the moon." Elias Mose looked up to the crest, which seemed like a great head and shoulders of the earth. "What am I s'posed to do if I see 'em?"

Murray drove along, bouncing across the bottom of a wash filled with stones the size of skulls, hanging on to the steering wheel with both hands, trying to keep the truck going in a straight line.

"Spook 'em," he said when they reached the other side.

"You mean like a ghost?"

"Like a bear," Murray said.

As they climbed through the piñon pine and entered the canyon that followed the creek, trees grew tighter along the edge of the road, blocking the moonlight, scraping down the sides of the truck. Half an hour later, they spotted Valerie's Jeep, gleaming like a rhinoceros at the trailhead.

From behind the seat, Murray pulled a flashlight and a denim jacket lined with fleece and handed them to Elias Mose, who was beginning to feel anxious about the deal.

"I don't know about this," he said. "I ain't no woodsman really."

"There's the trail." Murray grabbed the flashlight and pointed to an opening in the trees. "Like a sidewalk almost." With the light under his arm, he pulled a twenty-dollar bill from his wallet. "Paid in full, whether you find 'em or not."

Murray told Elias Mose to use the flashlight only when necessary, and not at all after he smelled their woodsmoke or saw their campfire.

"It won't be a big fire," Murray explained. "It won't be a white man's fire."

He slapped Elias Mose on the shoulder and laughed, but Elias Mose did not laugh. He growled like a bear for Murray and disappeared between the trees.

For a while, the trail was soft and wide, covered with a thick carpet of pine needles, but when it reached the creek and started climbing, Elias Mose put the flashlight in his pocket so he could use both hands to pull himself over large rocks and fallen trees. He understood why Murray could never reach the summit and felt sorry for him because his foot was missing.

As the moon climbed higher in the sky, he walked along through the forest like the other animals who made their way from place to place on the mountain that night, although Elias Mose did not see them. Eventually, the trail left the creek and switched back up a loose rock hillside to a ridge with no trees where Elias Mose sat down to rest because he was breathing heavily and his heart was crashing in his chest. He was at eight thousand feet. He was wearing tennis shoes. He was not a good hiker.

From the little ridgetop, he could see the summit not far above him, and the valley below, bathed in moonlight, sloping away into the night. He leaned back against the low sage and thought about his trip to the Holy Land, as his heart slowed down and his breathing returned to normal, and he noticed the small sounds around him. The whole sky pressed down on him as he traveled in his mind, over forests and great rivers, lighted cities stretched like frail open hands, then more mountains and water until he reached age-old Jerusalem, the walled city of Palestine. Like a huge magnet it pulled Elias Mose across the earth, as it had pulled so many others, to a place where they looked to the heavens in pure wonder, arms open, palms up, and gave themselves over to a mystery they could not put into words. Elias Mose looked up from his little ridgetop in the middle of Nevada and saw a sheet of clouds spreading halfway across the sky, crowding the moon. He stood up and started for the summit.

Murray, being the kind of guy who can't sit still for too

long, didn't sit still. After rubbing his thighs for a while and thinking like a beaver, he pulled a propane light from behind the seat and gimped around to the back of the truck, where he rummaged through the mess of tools and junk. He set up a workstation on the tailgate and started dismantling a lawn mower engine, huddled like a surgeon under a little tent of light.

Just below the summit, Elias Mose smelled smoke. He stopped like a deer, judging the wind and listening, watching for movement in his side vision. Without using his flashlight, he continued up the trail along the open slope, entering a stand of cedar and juniper growing low and gnarly from the high altitude and wind. As the trail disappeared, running off in every direction at once, he tripped on a piece of wood and fell flat on his chest. The ground was soft with duff and he was not hurt. But from that low angle he saw the glow of a fire, just a flicker now and then. He crouched, his eyes wide like a cat.

As he moved in, he saw two people and a little tent, plain as day in a small clearing. One of them got up, put a piece of wood on the fire, so Elias Mose inched forward from tree to tree, picking his steps carefully. At the edge of the trees he stopped and watched the women, who appeared to be wrestling on the edge of the firelight.

Elias Mose had never seen two women making love before. He'd seen pictures. He'd seen a couple movies. But never the real thing before his eyes. And although the light was not good, and the high altitude made his heart beat faster than usual and less oxygen was getting to his brain, he knew exactly what he was seeing.

At first he felt like an intruder, like he should turn around and walk away, having stumbled upon something that was none of his business, but he didn't. He picked up a stick, leaned against a pine tree, and snapped the stick over his knee. Nothing happened. The women did not hear him. So he moved a little closer and found a bigger stick, which he broke by whacking it against a little tree like a baseball bat. The women stopped. Then Elias Mose growled and shook the little cedar tree with both hands, like a bear, and he heard a giant explosion and the zipping sound of a bullet passing nearby.

He turned around and sprinted blindly, branches whipping his face, tumbling and losing the flashlight. Another shot was fired, so he turned and scrambled downslope, groping like a blind man until he reached a clearing, which turned out to be the little ridgetop where he'd rested on the way up. He recognized it. He could feel it.

When Murray heard the shots, he stopped working and started rubbing his thighs. He figured Miriam was doing the shooting because his wife didn't have a gun and couldn't shoot straight if she had one. Murray feared Elias Mose had been shot, so his mind started going so fast he could barely concentrate on the tiny carburetor parts he'd spread on an old dish towel—the small screws and rods and filter cones, the hairlike springs.

Every few minutes he stopped tinkering and listened. Finally Elias Mose showed up, panting like a hound dog, his eyes bulging, twigs in his beard. He grabbed Murray by the shoulder.

"You didn't tell me they had a gun," he said.

"I didn't know."

"I wouldn't've done it. Not for twenty bucks."

"You didn't get shot, did you?"

"No."

"Well, then. Did you see 'em?"

"I seen 'em."

"What was they doin'?"

"Sittin'." Elias Mose didn't have the heart to tell Murray

the truth. He couldn't begin to find the words. "They had a fire goin' and they was sittin'."

Murray wrapped his lawn mower parts in the dish towel and they took off down the road. An hour later they were back in Adaven, where Murray helped Elias Mose unload his shopping cart and showed him the bunkhouse, where he curled up under a thick pile of blankets on the bed and dreamed of Jerusalem. The old city rested on the mountain like an ancient crown. It was quiet and cold. From within the city walls, he heard a vague rumbling that seemed to emanate not from the blocks of stone or the dwellings or the many people who moved around inside. It came from the whole city itself, like a faint pulse barely heard through the heavy accumulation of centuries.

Snow started falling just before sunrise, and by the time Murray rolled out of bed there was already an inch on the ground. Valerie had still not come home. Murray looked out the living-room window, across the driveway toward the bunkhouse, and spotted Elias Mose pushing his shopping cart through the snow. By the time he put his clothes on and limped to the front door, Elias Mose was standing on the porch with his hands in his pockets.

"Where you goin'?" Murray asked.

"Jerusalem."

"You can't go to Jerusalem in the snow." Murray peered deep into the swirling storm.

But Elias Mose shook Murray's hand and took off down the driveway. He wouldn't accept a ride, not even to the main road. From the window, Murray watched him push his shopping cart into the storm until he disappeared completely. For several minutes Murray stood there, figuring he would reappear out of the snow as easily and smoothly as he'd slipped away, but he didn't.

By evening the weather had cleared, leaving half a foot of

wet snow on everything between the Sierras and Salt Lake City. A big, grinning moon broke through the clouds and lit up the whole country. Murray couldn't sleep much because he worried about Elias Mose, figuring he'd curled up under the weight of the storm and gone to sleep for good. Although Murray had only known Elias Mose for less than a day, he felt a bond between them. Maybe it was because Murray had never traveled much and he admired Elias Mose for his sense of adventure and his ability to move around like a wild mustang. Maybe it was the *way* he traveled, without much money, but with a drive that pulled him across the earth to mysterious places and an uncertain future. At dawn, Murray climbed into his truck and took off in search of Elias Mose.

He drove for a long time, slowing down for snow-covered bushes and rocks, checking for tracks. All the way to the paved road he went, where he made a wide loop in the sagebrush and spotted the shopping cart parked by the side of the highway, completely empty, snowless and gleaming in the sun. Murray got out of the truck and hobbled over to the cart. He looked around for a sign of what had happened, but it appeared that the cart had simply dropped out of the sky and landed there in the snow on the side of the road. Not a sound except the hollow rush the wind makes when it has nothing to blow against. Murray looked one way and then the other, along the road that curved up from the bottom of the valley in both directions like two slender wings. In the west, the moon had still not set. Murray stood there for a long time with one arm pointing to the sun and the other arm pointing to the moon and his head rolled back. He opened the palms of his hands to the sky and closed his eyes.

Then he bent over the shopping cart and scooped his arms through the empty basket, feeling for something—anything—to give him reason to believe Elias Mose had ever existed at all. Murray felt a hole in his belly as big as a bushel basket, as if someone had opened a spigot in the bottom of his boot and let the life run out of him. He wondered when Valerie would get home. He missed her deeply.

With one hand on the shopping cart, he watched a large silver truck approach from the west. It was still several miles away and moved silently, like a marble in a groove. As the truck rushed by, the driver waved and blew his horn in a spray of mist and grit. For a long time, Murray watched the truck grow smaller and smaller as it climbed toward the sky and finally shrank to a little point that hung above the eastern summit like a star.

A HARD WAY TO MAKE A HUNDRED BUCKS

We took off from Adaven on a full moon so we could drive without lights. It was me and Nelson, heading for the Test Site on a wager with Mickey Maxwell, who'd worked as a welder at Papoose Lake until they laid him off because we won the Cold War and there wasn't a need to explode atomic bombs underground anymore. That was just fine with Mickey because he married our sister and wasted no time getting her in a family way. And it was fine with me because I'd never seen a spaceship, even though I'd spent my whole life under the stars of that part of Nevada, where, according to Mickey, they came and went like clockwork.

Papoose Lake isn't a lake at all, but rather a huge alkali flat that *used* to be a lake before the days of the earliest Indians. Now the lake's a landing zone, with runways and underground hangars and a whole city under the sagebrush. Mickey told us about it, not because he simply wanted to tell a good story, but because we were family by then and he just had to let it out. Meanwhile, we paid him a wage well more than he was worth as a worker, figuring some of it would filter back on our sister and us, but he wasted more on welding supplies than ever filtered back in *any* direction. We asked him flat out to start helping more with things that needed doing, but he just shook his head. "Can't do it," he'd say. It made me and Nelson mad, especially Nelson because he was so willful and hotheaded to begin with, but we couldn't do much about it.

Mickey was a jack Mormon. Just like a jack*ass* looks something like a horse and a jack*rabbit* looks mostly like a rabbit, Mickey had the outward signs of a good Mormon except he wasn't as hardworking or reliable as a horse or tame as a regular rabbit. He lived with us under one roof only because he married our sister, Miriam, who was already weathered and somewhat past the point of getting married and having children. Like a wild cow running downhill, there wasn't a thing me or Nelson could do to stop her from falling directly in love for the first time in her life. We tried. Lord knows, we tried. We just couldn't understand how a man could live like that, living mostly off the labor of me and Nelson and off the love of our sister. So when he bet us a hundred bucks on the fact of there being spaceships at Papoose Lake, Nelson took him up on it.

As we pulled out of Adaven, Miriam and Mickey stood in the moonlight under the cottonwood tree. I watched them through the back window of the truck and I remember seeing the curve of Miriam's belly and wondering what would become of us. It wasn't any surprise. It's just the sight of them two together like that in the moonlight gave me the chills and churned up memories better left buried. My hands went cold. It froze my guts. I sat there turned around backward in my seat.

"Nelson," I said. "Miriam's gonna have a child."

"Jesus, Ed," he said. He waved his hand around like he was shooing a fly. I could tell by the look on his face that he'd been thinking it too, but he kept his eyes on the road. "Oh, Jesus."

That's all he said until he went completely quiet and we drove without saying a single word, rolling down out of sight and into the pitch darkness of Sandsprings Valley together.

With the lights off we headed up Cottonwood Creek, picking our way over rocks and through the washes. The trees glowed as if they had snow on them and patches of moonlight on the ground looked like snow, but it was August and I had my elbow out the window. Nelson had both hands on the wheel the whole way and he shifted into four-wheel drive near the summit, where the ground loosened and the creek fanned out across the road. He stopped the truck on the lip of the wash. We could barely see the other bank, and the water looked deep because it ran smooth as stone and reflected no moonlight.

Before I knew what was happening, Nelson revved the engine and lurched off the bank and we were bouncing and swerving across the creek, my head hitting the roof as we plowed down deep into the water and the tires of the truck grabbed for solid ground. We started to shimmy sideways with the current, water pouring up over the windshield and Nelson couldn't let go of the wheel to turn on the wipers, but he pulled us through and we hit the other bank flat on. It threw us forward and Nelson kept going, more out of nerves than anything else, until the water drained off the windshield and things came back into focus and we stopped.

With both hands still on the wheel, he said, "Miriam's gonna have a baby."

Just like that, like he'd been thinking it ever since we'd left Adaven. He sat there with his head cocked to the side, looking at me with his little eyes like he wanted me to tell him it wasn't true, but I couldn't.

"It's a large thought," I said.

"Hurts me to think about it."

"Then let's not think about it," I said.

And he said, "It ain't that simple. It gnaws at me."

We started down the road, much smaller on that side of the summit, and rougher and full of rocks. The trees grew tighter along the sides, blocking the moonlight and making it feel like driving through a tunnel, the branches of juniper and cedar scraping down the sides of the truck. Even though we'd been driving in the dark for over an hour and our eyes were accustomed to the lack of light, they'd still play tricks on us. "What's that?" I'd say, and Nelson would slow the truck and we'd lean forward and open our eyes wide to see more. "Just a shadow," he'd say, and we'd go on because it wasn't a time for talk. And that's the way we went until we broke out of the trees, into the rabbit brush and high sage on the washes above the valley.

It felt good to get out in the open. The moon was very bright and the road was smooth and we could relax again. The border of the Test Site was halfway up the slope of the next hills and we got there by an old jeep trail overgrown with sagebrush, just like Mickey'd told us. We found the fence topped with barbed wire and a sign by the Department of Defense saying RESTRICTED AREA, NO TRESPASSING BEYOND THIS POINT and a whole list of reasons and other signs telling us why we shouldn't go past the fence, but we did.

With bolt cutters Nelson snipped a hole big enough to squeeze through, and I folded it back so you couldn't tell it was cut. We took the field glasses and set out on foot for Paiute Mesa, not following any road or trail but simply cutting through the sagebrush toward the hill we could see in the distance. That's when we saw the first one. Heard it, that is, and then saw it. The sound was a low humming, a rumble like faraway thunder. It came from everywhere at once and there weren't any lights and me and Nelson hunkered down like something was about to hit us on the head until Nelson dropped his binoculars and pointed.

"There," he said. "Like a shadow."

And sure enough, I saw it too. Or rather, I saw *something* dark as the night itself, blocking the stars as it moved, reflecting no moonlight, heading straight for Papoose Lake. It was like seeing something that wasn't really there by seeing just a *sign* of it, like leaves moving on a tree are only the *sign* of blowing wind. The noise didn't slowly fade like a jet, but cut off like a spigot as it dropped over Paiute Mesa and left us standing in the dark together.

Around one o'clock we reached the top of the mesa, which wasn't really flat like a tabletop but was more like the back of an elephant, gentle and sloping and covered only with rock and ricegrass and low black sage. The moon had slipped down behind us as we rounded the crest enough to look down to the valley and then to Papoose Lake, where we saw the landing zone laid out in blue lights just like Mickey said.

We dropped down on our bellies and took turns with the binoculars. The earth was still warm from the hot sun that day and the heat waves made everything dance and swim, but it was clear enough—the blue lights, the tin buildings, the two spaceships sitting side by side at the far end of the runway. Like two crows on a hay bale they hunkered there, looking like nothing we'd ever seen before. They weren't sleek and smooth like I'd imagined, but more bulky and angular, built for the long haul through space. Then Nelson spotted an alien.

"It's a critter." He wouldn't give up the glasses.

"What's he look like?"

"Kinda like us. It looks like two legs, but shorter and more spindly, and the head looks bigger. It ain't a human."

I grabbed the glasses and sure enough, I saw a *something* dancing and weaving in the heat waves, heading for the tin shed, which no doubt led to the underground city Mickey talked about. He wore a white suit and his head might've been a little bigger than ours, but it could have been a helmet or a hat or just the heat waves playing tricks on me. When I lowered the binoculars and looked down, all I could see was two rows of blue lights and the dull reflection of a tin shed in the middle of a dry lake.

"It makes me feel kinda small," I said. I gave Nelson the glasses and laid down on my back, stretching my arms out and running my fingers into the dirt. I spread my legs and dug in the heels of my boots. For a minute I could have sworn I could feel the whole earth spinning, real slow, and Nelson stood up and said something, but I didn't hear him because I was looking at the stars and thinking of Miriam and Mickey and of all that'd happened since we first moved to Adaven.

It was a powerful feeling, like a dream or a prophecy that plowed up memories better left forgotten. We were just kids when our father named the place Adaven, which is "Nevada" spelled backward, because he believed the whole world was spinning backward on us. He said it as we buried our mother in the piñon pine less than two seasons from the time we'd moved there. "Everything's upside down," he'd say, when a good cow died for no good reason, or a hen suddenly stopped laying eggs, or when the horse was born with an extra leg. More than a hundred times he said it before he died, too, of a fast-growing tumor and left me and Nelson and Miriam to carry on as best we could. I was scared. I stretched out on my back, watching the stars move, wondering when it all would stop. I felt helpless and so small, not able to move a muscle. I couldn't get my mind away from it, until I heard Nelson talking again and felt him kick my hip with the side of his boot.

"Helicopter," he yelled.

I heard it thumping first and saw it come from behind a hill and dip into a canyon and disappear again. From the belly of the helicopter, a bright light shined down and lit up the desert like daytime. We ran off the hill and stopped in a group of junipers to catch our breath and listen, as it crisscrossed the mesa and headed off away from us. Like a couple of kids, me and Nelson hiked back to the truck, but when we got there we were surrounded by two sheriffs from Lincoln County, who arrested us for trespassing, handcuffed us, and put us in the backseat of their truck. I could see Nelson's jaw muscles flexing, and I knew if it wasn't for his hands being tied behind his back, he would've lurched forward and strangled one of them. Instead, he just sat there looking out the window.

We drove through the valley and over the summit and went crashing through Cottonwood Creek, me and Nelson bouncing and rolling around in the backseat like a couple of clay pigeons because we couldn't hold on to anything. We drove right past Adaven, just a quarter mile off the road. The cabin lights were on, unusual for two in the morning, and smoke rose straight up from the chimney, fanning out in the moonlight. In Caliente, everybody was sleeping as they put us in the county jail.

When I called home, the phone rang and rang until Mickey finally answered, all out of breath like he'd run from a far distance.

"Hello, Mickey," I said. "We're in the county jail."

And he said, "She's havin' it, Ed. Right now she's havin' it."

"Miriam's having the baby?" I said, and Nelson went down on his knees and started slapping the floor.

"Oh, Jesus," he said, "not now, Miriam."

Meanwhile, Mickey went back to help Miriam, who I

could hear in the background, hollering from time to time and I heard Mickey yelling back at the phone, "She's havin' it, Ed," or "It's coming," and one time he yelled for help, but there wasn't a thing me or Nelson could do from Caliente. Nelson got up off the floor and stood next to me, pounding the doorjamb with the side of his fist.

I kept calling for Mickey, but of course he couldn't hear me, and Nelson walked back and forth, making comments about Mickey and throwing his arms around like he was beating off a bunch of bugs. "The guy's a bum," he'd say, or "the horses are all gonna die," or "the whole place is gonna sink right into the ground," none of which happened, but then everything went quiet on the phone. Miriam quit wailing and Mickey quit hollering and all of a sudden I heard the crying of a baby, which was very peculiar, to hear such a sound coming from our own cabin over the telephone lines to Caliente.

"It's the baby," I said, and gave Nelson the phone.

"Jesus," he said. That's all he said for a long time, until I had the phone again and Mickey finally came back, telling me it was a boy baby.

"It's a boy," I told Nelson.

"Is it whole?" he said, spreading both hands out in front of him like he was holding a watermelon. It put me in mind of the horse born with an extra leg and I just stood there without being able to move or speak.

"Is the baby whole?" Nelson asked again.

"They ain't said it ain't."

"Ten fingers. Ten toes. Arms and legs, two and two?"

"I don't know. I don't know."

Mickey got back on the phone and promised to be at the jailhouse by noon, but didn't get there until three. And when he did show up, he was in such a state over the baby and anxious to get home again, we could hardly talk to him. He paid our bail with a hundred-dollar bill. He made sure we saw it, tapping it on the counter and running it back and forth before sliding it across the desk.

"One hundred dollars," he said, and that's all he said about the bet we'd made. All the way home we drove fast without talking about what'd happened to me and Nelson that night. They named the baby Varlin, after our father, and he was healthy and round-faced and the first baby ever born in Adaven.

We figured Mickey'd give up welding altogether and concentrate more on cows, but he didn't. He didn't get more serious about life, harder working or more regular like most men do. However, something did happen that changed the whole picture and brought us together in a way we never expected and never knew before. It might've been the baby, partially. Or it might've been the incident at Papoose Lake, because it made me feel so small compared to the whole earth and the distance to the farthest stars. When you live all alone in the middle of nowhere, depending only on yourself for everything, you come to believe you're bigger than you really are, that you can get along without the help of anybody else, and that the whole world ends at the farthest point on the horizon. It simply ain't true.

When we finally sat down to lunch that day, Miriam blessed the meal, except she carried on at length to Our Heavenly Father about the importance of things not normally included in a meal blessing at our place. "Our Heavenly Father," she said, "we thank thee for such a fine and solid cabin which keeps us warm in winter and cool in summer. We ask thee for patience, to see our way clear to acceptin' folks who are different from ourself," and I knew she was talking about Mickey and how me and Nelson hadn't seen him as a regular member of the family. Miriam held Varlin close to her, and he looked up with eyes as clear as creek water, as if he understood every word she was saying, even though he didn't. "Give us the gift of hospitality," she said. "Give us a feeling of community."

I remember the lunch very clearly, not only because of what Miriam said and not because of the food, which was no different from all the lunches we had. Through most of the meal Nelson kept his head down and ate slowly, which was uncommon for him because he usually ate and spoke at the same high rate. I think that's when he finally came to realize there wasn't much sense in fighting something bigger than he was. For the remainder of the day, he didn't talk and I knew he was busy thinking about all that'd happened, and he didn't say a single word about Mickey.

Before I went to sleep that night, I read from the Book of Mormon because I'd finished a good story by Louis L'Amour the night before and the next day was Sunday. I read from Nephi, who spoke of endurance. "Blessed is he that endureth to the end," he said, and I figured that all of us had certainly endured more than the normal person and that we'd most likely continue to the end. Bad feelings, like old bones, don't really stay buried in the earth forever. All of them quietly work their way back to the surface until they reach the sun and the air again.

From out in the corral, I heard a calf bawling like it missed his mother, but a sound like that is common on a farm as long as it doesn't persist, so I kept reading until my eyes got heavy and burned for sleep. But the calf kept bawling. I didn't want him to wake up Orrin, and Nelson was sleeping in his chair across from me, looking peaceful and quiet at last, so I checked the corral and sure enough, the mother cow had broken out and headed for the alfalfa. I saddled up and rode around behind her. She stood still and silvery in the moonlight, but when she saw me coming she started running and bellowing like I was coming to cut her throat.

By the time I finally got her heading back home, we were half a mile out in the valley. I saw the lights of the shop where Mickey was working, and a trail of smoke from the cabin where the rest were sleeping. That's when I heard another low rumbling like faraway thunder, almost too low to hear, and when I stopped and tried to listen, the whole sky went quiet. But as soon as I moved out and my mind got to wandering, I heard it again, coming and going from every direction at once. And from the corner of my eye, I saw something dark moving through the night, but when I looked straight at it, there was nothing there but so many stars just vibrating against the sky.

WATER BABY

When Evan opened the door of Duman's cabin, it smelled bad and no one answered. He checked his pockets for the beaded bottle the old man had given him and wondered if it had anything to do with Duman not being home or with the ambulance that had just left the meadow. Past the big red fir he raced with elbows out, lips pressed tight and one sneaker untied dragging laces through the sagebrush and greasewood just like last time. He headed for Goat Rock, a four-story granite slab slanting up out of Horsethief Meadow at just the right angle so you can climb it on all fours, but Duman wasn't there. Up the rock the easy way he climbed from the side and cried to the sky like the old Indian had told him. Tough as a badger, Evan thought, just like Duman said, it took twelve shots till that old bugger's lip covered his snarling teeth and his nose hit the dirt.

Evan cupped his hands around his mouth.

"Duman!" he yelled across the meadow and into the flat gray sky, but the forest swallowed the sound. He slid down the rock and ran back to Duman's cabin, where he walked softly across the redwood floor—the old man's house always felt like a church—and placed the beaded bottle back on the shelf behind rock-filled jars and salt and pepper shakers. Before he reached the door again, he stopped and put his hand on the woodstove. It was bone cold. He could not figure why Duman had disappeared without saying a word. Then Evan walked back to the far corner of the cabin, took the bottle off the shelf again, and ran home.

When he got there, his mother was on her knees in the yard, splitting kindling for dinner. She knew already that Duman had left in the ambulance for the second time that year and also that Evan would be all worked up wondering if he would ever come back again. Half an hour earlier, she'd called the sheriff when she saw the old man standing like a deer on the edge of the meadow. He'd been missing for forty hours. As Evan raced around the woodpile, she put down the hatchet and stayed kneeling in the dirt.

"Is Duman gonna die this time, Ma?" he said.

"I told you once, I told you a thousand times," she told him, "Duman won't die unless he wants to, but he doesn't want to, that's all." She smiled as if she could tell the future.

Evan and Duman had been close friends since the snow melted in late May. Before that, Duman drove places almost every day and their paths never really crossed, even though the old man lived just a stone's throw up the river. The first trip to the hospital slowed him down good and nearly killed him from coughing up blood. Although Mrs. Cook didn't like the idea of Evan spending so much time with Duman, there wasn't much she could do about it since no other children lived in the little subdivision and Woodfords was eight miles away down the canyon.

Because her husband had died the year before, leaving her to carry on as she could in a one-room cabin with a seven-year-old boy, Mrs. Cook was grateful to Duman for acting like a father to Evan, but she worried about the kinds of things he was teaching him, Indian stories that made his mind go off in a million directions. But most folks liked Duman, or rather they had better things to say about him than about the other Washoes around, probably because he worked most of his life as a janitor for the school and people like an Indian who works eight hours a day at a regular job. And they liked him too because he was old, well over eighty, and the oldest Washoe in Toiyabe County.

Back to Duman's cabin Evan ran without stopping, wondering all the way if it was something *he* had done, or had *not* done, that caused the old man to disappear in the forest. He stopped at the little gate and ran his hand over the place where Duman's own hand, from years of careful opening and closing, had worn the wood smooth and shiny like an old piece of furniture. He closed and latched the outhouse door, which had blown open in a wind, and he looked around to make sure everything was in its proper place, figuring the smallest thing out of order would prevent the old man's return. From the table he picked up a big pinecone and threw it as far as he could toward the river.

Inside the cabin, Evan found the half-cleaned trout on the counter by the woodstove where Duman had left it. They'd planned to have trout for breakfast the day he vanished. He wrapped the mess in newspaper and cleaned the counter. Then he sat in his chair, the old wooden chair that Duman had named as Evan's chair, not only because it was smaller than his own, but also because it was the only other chair in the cabin. With both elbows on the armrests, Evan sat holding the beaded bottle, rolling it between his fingers and listening to the aspens, remembering the first time Duman had showed him the bottle, at five in the morning—Duman's favorite time of day and Evan's too—just before the sun comes up when everything is bathed in a pearly half-light.

The old man had groaned with tightness as he scraped a step stool across the dull redwood floor. One step at a time he climbed, like old folks do, reaching way back behind a clutter of stone-filled jars and salt and pepper shakers. In his fingers he held it, about an inch high and shaped like a little milk bottle, completely covered in colorful beads. He handed it to Evan and sat in his own chair by the stove. "It's hard work," he'd said, "to bead a bottle so small. You see, you can't tell where it starts and where it stops 'cause my mamma she was the best beadworker from Reno to Bishop and she was famous for that. If you turn it 'round and 'round you see how the colors look like they're moving. That's peyote design."

"What's a peyote?" Evan had said, rolling the bottle in the palm of his hand.

"It's the way the beads are on the bottle, from medicine the Indian doctor gives for your eyes. If you have trouble with your eyes, it makes you see better."

Alone in the cabin Evan sat, listening to the river, waiting for Duman. He stayed there for three days, going home only to sleep and eat. The rest of the time, he sat in his chair or on the woodpile and watched the road through the meadow.

When the old man returned, walking in slowly along the river like a deer at dusk, Evan was waiting for him, sitting on the woodpile.

"Hey, black boy," Duman said as he came through the gate, "what you doin' in my woodpile?"

Really only half black by blood—with Mrs. Cook being mostly Portagee anyway—Evan did look black. Duman's father was a black man too, a ranch hand named Barber, but no one ever asked Duman directly. Folks could see that his face was darker than any other Indian's. And that may be the reason Evan and Duman fell in so close together in so short a time, not that they were half black so much as that they were simply half something and half something else.

"I'm tryin' to catch a marmot," Evan said and his face felt hot. "With my hands if I'm quick enough from behind like this." He crouched and moved slowly forward with his wrists together, fingers outstretched. "Like this I'd get him." He pounced. "Like that."

Duman walked to the cabin. Like a penguin, Evan thought, back and forth from side to side with each step, just a little. The old man wore boots at the bottom of his bowed-out legs, curved from riding horses when he was younger.

"You won't catch no marmot in a woodpile," Duman said without turning around. "You'd have to move the whole pile stick by stick and then he be gone." He waved for Evan to follow him and disappeared inside the cabin.

In his chair by the Franklin stove Duman sat with his arms on the armrests and his hands moving always from side to side over the shiny leather and brass tacks. Those hands had made the leather look smooth and strong from years of thoughtful stroking. Evan wondered, too, if the leather had somehow changed the hands.

Duman rested his head back against the chair and looked somewhere on the wall or along the ceiling without blinking. When Duman got quiet like that, Evan watched his eyes, the way they seemed to lie in pockets like a puppet's eyes, as if they were made of glass. It reminded him of his own father, who had the same look about him the last time Evan saw him lying in a hospital bed, shortly before he died. It was a look of fear that showed up only in the eyes and couldn't be covered up. Not until Evan saw this in Duman did he connect it with his father or with death at all.

"Why does a person want to die?" Evan asked.

"Nobody *wants* to die." Duman leaned forward in his chair.

"But when a man is finished his work, he lays down to rest on his own."

"Just like that? You just lay down?"

"Just like that."

"How can you tell when a person is done with work?"

"It's one of them things," Duman said. "Hard to say what it looks like, but when you see it, you know what it is. It's like a water baby."

Duman stroked the armrests of his chair, and Evan knew a story was brewing because that was the way the old man always started. He would mention something Evan never heard of before and then just sit there like everything was perfectly normal.

"What's a water baby anyway?"

Like a magician, Duman opened both hands and showed them to the boy.

"You know," he said, "in Jesus Christ time people sometime look like a cloud?" Evan watched the old man's hands without answering. "You know people in them days had miracles?"

"Yeah."

"Well that's like water babies. But only *some* people see them. They're spirits of them that died and they're smart too. When a white man comes they turn like a cloud and then sometimes they turn like us." Duman slapped his barrel chest. "Solid."

"You ever seen 'em?" Evan asked.

"Oh, I see 'em. They're just like people, only small, about this small." He held his palm out over the floor. "Papoose like you. Small and gentle and they walk with their head down and cry like babies in the forest. Maybe you see 'em too, if you don't have a problem with your eyes."

Before dawn the next day, Evan showed up at Duman's

cabin. Duman had been awake already for more than an hour, busy in the shed getting ready to go fishing. But when the boy opened the door to the cabin and saw that Duman was gone, he froze stiff for a few seconds, unable to take his hand off the door, only his eyes moving back and forth looking for a sign of where the old man might be. Then he turned and ran for the back gate, heading for Goat Rock.

"Hey, boy!" Duman yelled and Evan stopped like he'd hit a tree. "Let's go fishin'."

With the willow pole swaying back and forth in front of him, up the wooden steps the old man started. Evan fell in behind him, through the gate and down the old two-track road that saw the start of all the walks those two took that year. Down to the river they went, following a path that snaked around the willows and wild rose. Only the hilltops had sun, and the air was very still and cold by the water. The river was full of rocks. Then Duman stopped and hooked his arm around the branch of an aspen.

"What's the matter?" Evan said. He thought the old man was in trouble.

"Badger." Duman straightened up and pointed. The badger was lying alongside the trail, his stubby legs sticking straight out like table legs and big hooked claws spread wide, grasping the air. He had no marks on him, no signs of a fight with any critter slightly tougher or more wily, if a creature like that even exists. No bullet holes. It appeared that the badger had simply stopped moving while he was walking down the trail, as if somebody had opened a little plug in his belly and his life drained out all at once.

"What killed him?" Evan said.

"Don't know." Duman nudged the badger with the toe of his boot. "He jus' stopped for no reason."

They stood over the dead animal without moving and without talking. The boy crouched down and touched the badger with his finger. Then he carefully stroked its grizzled fur with the flat of his hand, tracing the broad, white stripes from the crown of its head, back along the length of its muscled body.

"When I was young, I killed a badger," Duman said, even though he'd told the story before. "Took twelve shots to kill him. Never forget it. That bugger stood there snarlin' at me under a hot sun, showin' his teeth and kind of hissin' like a wind in the pine trees, lookin' straight at me with little black eyes. I shot him a few times and he didn't even jerk, jus' showed more teeth and got more angry, so I shot again and the bullets passed through him like he was a cloud even though I know I hit him. After a while, I loaded up and shot again to show him who's boss and I hit him right in the top of the skull. All of a sudden his eyes started swimmin' around and he closed his mouth and laid still, lookin' at me like he *knew* it was all over and it made me feel bad. I left him alone on the road, breathin' heavy, but when I came back, he was gone. He died someplace else, someplace of his own choosin'. Funny how some things stay with you all your life, things that seemed so little when they first happened."

Evan fished around in his pocket, pulled out the beaded bottle, and handed it to Duman.

"Here," he said. "I don't really need it no more," even though he remembered clearly what Duman had said when he'd given him the bottle. "So now it belong to you and not me," the old man had told him, "but you have to give it to somebody else. And don't wait eighty years to do it."

Duman smiled and pressed the little bottle into the boy's hand. "You hold it for me now," he said. He knew what Evan was trying to do even better than Evan himself knew and he laughed, but not a big laugh; he just squinted his pearly eyes and his belly shook a few times until he started coughing and that's when Evan saw blood for the first time. Duman saw it too, plain as day on the back of his hand, pure, bright red, like a crimson berry. On the side of his jeans he wiped it off like he'd wipe a spot of motor oil or fish gut, but Evan could tell that the old man was worried because his eyes flitted from side to side and looked like they were made of glass.

"Let's fish," Duman said, and he lumbered off like a bear that had caught the scent of humans. Evan followed him around granite boulders and dead snags until they reached their favorite spot, a wide pool where the river changed directions before picking up speed and spilling off down the canyon. The sun had finally climbed down the steep canyon wall and warmed their faces. Evan hunkered next to Duman and rubbed his hands together. About ten feet from the bank, a large cutthroat trout snaked against the current, green and yellow and red, shimmering in the sun.

Evan baited the hook, as usual, pulling a big hula worm from the coffee can, pushing it along the shaft of the hook and looping it a couple times around the barb. As usual, Duman said, "I hear him cryin'," speaking of the worm.

"Like a baby in the forest," Evan replied, even though he heard nothing, and the words had become, over time, a kind of incantation they recited, like a prayer or a good luck charm, every time they fished.

They caught the one they were after, a seven-pounder that Evan would never forget, even though he'd catch many more in his lifetime. He held the fish in both hands as it gulped for air and its gills snapped shut, smooth and colorful as treasure in the morning sun. Back along the river they went, Evan out front, carrying the fish on a stringer. Every once in a while he'd stop to dip the trout into the river, scanning the ridge of the canyon until Duman caught up. The old man coughed from time to time, and Evan kept thinking of something he could do or say to bring him around, but he just kept hiking along the river, trying to pick the easiest route, pushing forward over boulders and around the willows, heading home.

At the cabin, Duman took the fish and told Evan to check in with his mother. The boy ran straight home through the sagebrush and greasewood without following the road, but by the time he explained everything to his mother and made it back to Duman's cabin, he saw the fish on the counter by the sink and the old man was gone. Straight for the toolshed he ran, picturing the familiar, rounded shape of his friend in the half-light of the musty shed, hearing his soft voice, but the latch was closed from the outside. He ran for Goat Rock, the only other place he'd be, saying *Duman's dead Duman's dead* with each breath, over the yellow grass of the meadow, his leg muscles burning and his heart crashing in his chest. Sure enough, the old man sat with his back against the rock.

"I ain't dead," Duman said. He smiled and patted the ground next to him for Evan to sit down.

The two of them sat with their legs straight out, looking across the meadow to the high peaks of the crest. Duman rested his hands open in his lap.

"Listen," he said. "Listen to the sound the aspens make."

"Like little bones shakin'," Evan said.

"And up there, the sound of wind in the red fir."

"Like the hissin' of a badger."

"Jus' close your eyes and listen," Duman whispered. "Don't be afraid."

"I ain't afraid."

Evan rested his head back against the big granite rock and closed his eyes. He put his hand in his pocket and found the beaded bottle, listening to the crackle of pine needles as the old man shifted his weight. He sat and listened until he'd heard every sound the forest can make. He heard every combination of wind and creature and tree, not something he could put into words, but something he *knew* and could feel, as if everything around him had slipped into the right place all at once.

A soft cry came from the far end of the meadow where aspens curved up to the crest and Duman heard it, too, because Evan opened his eyes and saw the old man smiling. It was a kind of whimper that came with the wind, rising and falling as if carried on water. Not like a song exactly, it had melody, comforting like a lullaby or the rush of a river, but frightening too. When it finally quit, Evan sat there without moving and without really knowing what made the sound, figuring it could have been a redtail hawk or the bending of a big tree in the wind, but feeling deep inside that it was something much more than that.

They got back on their feet and Duman stood with his hands out in front of him like he was ready to lead a symphony. He looked at Evan in a way that made him feel like the old man was seeing right into the muscle of his heart.

"You see?" Duman said. That's all he said, as if everything—all the deep mystery of the forest, the grace of leaning trees, the reason water runs where it does, or wind, the rhythm of beetles running wild under the bark of rotting logs—as if everything had suddenly come into focus. And although Evan nodded like he *did* see, he really didn't. Not completely. Not yet.

They walked back to the cabin and ate the fish they'd caught, which turned out to be the best-tasting fish in Evan's life and a fish he'd never forget, even though he did eat one more with Duman before the old man died three weeks later.

It was on the second day of the first snow, just before dawn. Duman headed straight for the river and laid down with his head against an old aspen tree until the sun broke over the canyon wall and warmed his face. He stretched his legs out and crossed his ankles. He folded his arms on his chest. And that's just the way Evan found him a few hours later, covered with a dusting of snow, his feet a few inches from the edge of the water, lying there as if someone had pulled a little plug in the bottom of his boots and his life had simply drained out and flowed downstream.

Even before Evan reached him—even before he saw the smoke of his own breath curling up in front of his eyes as he whispered the word *Duman,* and before he saw the snow like powdered sugar on the old man's legs and chest, on his head and hands, his face the same color as the stone of the canyon, as if it had been carved from that stone—Evan knew he was dead. He sat down next to him and watched the river for a good long time, until the sound of the river seemed to be coming from inside his head and the ice-cold water ran right through him, until everything around him lost its color and shape and pointed in every direction at once. Then he went home and told his mother.

When the ambulance came again, he didn't run. For the first time, he didn't wonder what he might have done, or not done, to make things happen that day. Instead, he walked to Goat Rock and climbed it from the side, sitting cross-legged on top, watching the meadow and the shadow of clouds on the meadow moving like great old buffalo until the sun touched the hills and they disappeared for good. Shadows deepened. He expected something to happen—a great noise or a tremor in the earth—something to mark the end of Duman, like the last big note of a symphony gives a *feeling* of ending. But there was nothing. From the far distance, a raven flew in a straight line toward him, flapping its wings once in a while and soaring overhead on its way somewhere. He pressed his eyes shut and listened to the faint sounds of the forest, feeling his own life slipping forward like a field mouse without shaking the grass. Nothing else happened. Everything was real nice and quiet.

MUD BRICK

I stand by the fire and talk to a brick. I don't talk to the *brick* exactly, but rather to the man who made it, Mr. Lindsey Blossom. I hold it in one hand and use the other to help explain certain details, the contour of things, the anger I feel, or simply to mark the rhythm of my speech. Sometimes I put my ear very near the brick. Give me a sign, I say. I listen very carefully and wait.

There is a history of this brick that starts when the earth's crust is cooling. For millions of years, brick history is boring. Mountains heave and fall, spiny creatures cast fossils, and flies strike their final pose in amber. The huge lake that covers Nevada slowly shrinks, leaving a pocket of mud fed by deep springs, shaded only by sagebrush. Wild mustangs stumble in and slowly decompose. Wagon trains sink out of sight. And finally one day Lindsey drops down on his knees and scoops the mud up, pressing it into the corners of old boards to form bricks that dry in the sun. There is something of Lindsey in my brick, a drop of his sweat maybe, the curve of his thumb, or simply the echo of a song he sang that day. When I talk to the brick, I talk to Lindsey.

This is my survival camp. This cabin is all I have, my truck, these few trees, and the river that rolls from the high meadows all year long. Fifteen years ago I came here because of him, forty miles from my nearest neighbor, far from my old friends. He was the handsomest man I'd ever met, with black, tousled hair and a pair of watchful, anxious eyes. His skin was as soft as the curve of the earth and he spoke to me like he spoke to the wind, in measured tones, with a rhythm that ran as true as water. But he was an Indian, a Shoshone, and I sent him back into the cold night of that high desert town when he came courting me. And by the time I realized what I had done, he was gone.

He killed himself. He curled up quietly alongside his house and pulled one last breath from the barrel of a revolver in the late afternoon, leaving a big mess and a hand-drawn note that said nothing about me.

I've grown tired of being alone and of all the hard work, and I've nearly disabled myself from a fall, so I'm suffering. I broke my arm and dislocated my shoulder. I have to shift the truck with my left hand. I don't sleep well, so I go to bed early and that's when I feel most alone. In the cold and quiet time before I fall asleep, the whole story comes alive again and washes over me. I remember some and then I dream some, and these days the remembering and the dreaming are mingled, but it doesn't matter. Each time I remember the story, or dream it, I see the smallest details, the white moons of his fingernails, the smell of sagebrush after a rain, and I feel the wind in the valley against my face. Lindsey says amazing things sometimes. "You can never cross a river in the same place twice," he says. And amazing things happen in my dreams.

It was a bone-cold night, windless, and I was curled up under a pile of blankets when I heard a knocking at my bedroom window. I rolled out of bed and opened the curtains. Lindsey stood outside my window holding a brick in one hand, pointing to it with the other.

We sat in the kitchen.

"I love you, Rachel," he said, and he pushed the brick across the table to me. Slightly larger than a normal brick, it was a yellowish color, irregular and bumbly on one side.

"For me?" I said, touching it with my fingertips.

"For you," he said. "It's from my dream house, six bricks thick, to keep cool in summer and warm on nights like this."

"It's two in the morning," I said. "This is *not* going to work."

And I sent him away. I closed my door and sent him back into the cold night, but I watched from my window as he walked down the dirt road, into the yellow light of the water works building, where he stopped and hooked his arm around a little apple tree and waltzed with the frozen limbs. He dipped deeply on one knee. Then he stopped and gave me a little sign with two fingers before folding back into the darkness, and that was the last time I ever saw the man.

I throw the brick, heave it like a shot put over the woodpile, into the river. The river is only a foot deep and a few yards wide and I watch the brick from time to time, wavering yellow against the current, catching sunlight like a cutthroat trout. All day long it sits on the sandy bottom, cold and breathless, as I go about my chores. I never forget where it is. At night I check up on it with a flashlight. The brick has not moved.

"You can never cross a river in the same place twice," Lindsey said.

So I take off my clothes, my right arm in a sling like the wing of a featherless bird. The cool wind finds my breasts, stiffens my nipples and runs between my thighs, under my arms, along my spine like the finger of a man I once knew. Leaving the flashlight behind, I step into the river, numbing cold even in late summer. My feet roll slowly over rounded rocks until I stop midstream and look up beyond the lidless stars, deep into the eyes of a madness I know has grown in me. Why have I come here and stayed alone so long? What chance do I have to survive this winter, the slip of an ax, or another hurtful fall?

My legs fold delicately beneath me like scissors and I sit waist deep in water, my eyes wide like a cat when it hears something it cannot see, catching light from stars that burned years and years ago. The river surges against me, bringing with it all manner of unknown things from who knows where. I feel sticks and small stones. Long weeds snake along my legs. Probing currents touch me and move on as I stand again and walk evenly on sand to the far bank before turning and returning to the very spot I started, crossing the river in exactly the same place, twice. But I know I have failed. As the stars I see are not the stars at all, but simply the burning image of a star that once was, so is any spot on a river not the river twice, and so is my love of a man no longer the love I came here to secrete.

Before breakfast, I reach into the cold water and pull out the brick. I set it on the cookstove next to the coffeepot, where it steams and hisses until the moisture bubbles out from the nooks and crannies, until the whole brick becomes warm and then much too hot to touch. It does not crack. Unlike me, it can only be what it was fashioned to be. It holds the fossils frozen, the raised grain of weathered wood, the crown of his thumb. He used the rhyolite, the quartz, the feldspar. He knew what creatures had given their spines to become the sand of time. He knew then, as I know now, that love creates itself endlessly, like the fury of an atom bomb. By noon, the fire dies and everything goes back to normal.

I laugh out loud.

I'm a mess. I stand in front of the mirror nailed to a cottonwood tree, my hair greasy, gray and unbrushed. With my good hand, I stretch the skin on my face, pulling it down over my cheekbones, back to my temples, ironing out the wrinkles around my eyes. I look at my hands, nicked and cut, callused and dirty, and I shake my head. These are not a woman's hands. What will I do?

I put on a dress. Yes, I have a dress, a slick black thing with spaghetti straps I keep for when I have to look good. Ha! I wash my hair and wear gloves that reach to my elbows to cover my ugly hands. I sing a song about Lindsey and about his brick, a song that starts way back when the crust of the earth was cooling and ends right here with me. It could be a love song. It might be a lullaby or a rhapsody, but it tells the whole story of how we met on the steps of the courthouse in a small town in the middle of nowhere. The song will tell how we fell in love before we even spoke to each other. I explain, in poetic terms, the fact that he was an Indian from Duckwater and I was a white woman from Tonopah and how I just couldn't bring myself to be seen with him in public because I was afraid of what people would say. Small towns are much different than big cities, you know.

Lord, have mercy!

I walk as I sing. From the cabin to the river, I carry his brick and sing about where it came from and how he made it and why he gave it to me.

I carry the memory of your
dance with an apple tree.
I carry the weight of your small monument of mud,
enduring the heat and the cold,
as you do.

I step into the river and push against the current until I reach a sandy spot, where I sit down and let the water fill my dress. Then I take a deep breath and lie back, watching the water skim over my face like time in fast motion. I want to sit up and take a breath, but I resist.

Then I sit straight up, clawing at the sky, gasping for air.

I listen. There's not a soul around. When my breathing slows down, I stand like a deer that catches the scent of something it cannot see. Not one movement. No sound. Just the way I like it.

THE BEAR HUNTERS

Judy opened the cabin door just wide enough to poke her head outside, sniffing the wind and turning back inside with eyes as wide as a cat when it hears something it cannot see. She touched her fingertips to her lips.

"Oh, Dean," she said, "it's eerie out there."

"Just the snow," I said, it's being late November with snow falling since daybreak. "The forest only *sounds* different."

"Ha! It's more than sound." She picked up one of the cats and sat down cross-legged on the floor next to the woodstove. "I ain't leavin'."

An hour later we finally left for Reno. I promised, several times, that it would be our last visit to the Forest Service office until the snow melted next spring.

"*Very* weird vibes," she said as we rolled down off the mountain, sitting there staring out the window with her whole body turned and tucked away against the door. Looking back, of course, she was right. We should have stayed at the cabin.

Four thousand feet below us, an hour's drive down the canyon in the flat of Nevada, Mitsy Thornbek stood at the teller's window in the Great Basin Bank and withdrew nine thousand dollars from her account, just as she had done every month for nearly a year, although we did not know this fact until the bear hunters told us when they showed up at our cabin after the big snow. Mitsy put the money in her purse and drove home in a green Toyota. A widow for eight years, she was excited about getting married the next day to Mr. Orrin McCutcheon from Saint George, Utah.

Unknown to Mitsy, Orrin was busy renting a camper at Camper Land in Reno. He wore a blue suit and very shiny shoes. There's a big sign along the road south of Reno that says *Camper Land* in silver letters with silver tabs that quake like aspen leaves and sparkle in the sun when the wind blows. Towering over the sign is a huge statue of Paul Bunyan with an ax on his shoulder and acres and acres of campers lined up side by side at his feet for as far as you can see, thousands of them.

Judy and I avoid cities altogether, especially Reno. We feel clumsy in Reno and never go there except to visit Ernie Wucker at the Forest Service office because they were ready to build a logging road within spitshot of our cabin and take all the trees they could grab along the way, including the granddaddy of them all: the Old Man we call him, the biggest lodgepole pine on the mountain. He measures more than seventy-six inches in diameter four feet off the ground, his trunk covered with thick green moss so deep and soft it feels like fur. Sometimes we stand with our arms stretched around him, especially when things start closing in on us. The Old Man has a heartbeat.

As we drove to Reno and cruised by Camper Land in our old beater truck with a cracked windshield, Judy didn't say a word about the Old Man or about the big statue of Paul Bunyan like she usually did. She looked out the window, lost in thought.

"What's the matter?" I finally said, and she said, "I'm tired, Dean. Tired of fightin' the whole government and gettin' nowhere."

We'd been through this one before. Judy just shifted around in her seat and watched Camper Land go by. For a few months she'd been talking about moving back to Montana if things didn't work out. I didn't want to think about it.

By the time we reached the Federal Building parking lot, Judy started combing my hair with her fingers, trying to straighten it out and flatten it down with the palm of her hand.

"Jesus Christ, Dean," she said.

"It's just hair. It don't matter."

But it did. After having our stuff inspected at the main door to make sure we weren't bringing in a bomb, Judy asked the guard if he was *paranoid,* which led to *me* having to empty *my* pockets into a little tray while he ran a metal detector up and down my body, under my arms and around my boots, which had steel toes that set the thing screaming so I had to take off my boots and show the guy my dirty socks, which smelled like bad fish, while Judy stood there fanning her nose, saying, *Wheewee, boy!* Then the guy returned my things in the tray, all except the Chapstick, which he opened to make sure it was really full of lip stuff, and Judy said, "Ain't you gonna check his butthole, mister?"

"She's just kidding," I said. With my eyes I begged for mercy and we took off down the hall.

As always, Mr. Wucker smiled when he saw us. Judy says the kids at school probably called him Wucker the Fucker and that if his parents had changed their last name, he would have turned out different. I doubt it. I dreamed of knocking his teeth out, and by the looks of his teeth, I think somebody else had the idea before me, somebody with a little more moxie, somebody with a fist the size of a shovel.

"My tree-hugging friends," he said with both arms out like a grandfather. On his desk, he had a big chunk of granite shaped like sawtooth mountains with the words *Engineers Move Mountains* engraved on it.

We went right to work. We had maps. We had USGS maps, fifteen-minute topographical maps, and hand-drawn maps. We had copies of the original field notes handwritten by the first white men to walk the place with transit and chain in 1847, all to show we'd done our homework. We showed him a photograph of me and Judy and the Old Man, taken in the spring with the willows and wild rose in the background.

"Big lodgepole," Wucker said. "Must be fifteen thousand board feet."

"Board feet my ass," Judy said.

We explained how the Old Man was special, not only to us but to the whole forest, because he was so old. We told him we were not trying to *stop* the logging road, just as we wouldn't try to stop the wind or slow the shift of one season into the next. We showed how the road could be moved to a nearby ridge, cheaper and safer to drive with big trucks. Wucker hadn't ever seen the ridge because he'd never actually *been* there.

Then he said something very strange. He sat back on the front of his desk and looked around like he was seeing something mysterious in his side vision, but every time he turned his head there was nothing there, only the vague shadow of something moving away. Judy gave me the elbow.

"You know," he said, "to go back now and change things would cost taxpayers more money, unnecessarily." He folded his arms on his chest and smiled.

I didn't know what he was getting at, but I had a funny feeling, so I said, "*How much* more?"

He sat down and started poking his little calculator and

looking up at the ceiling and then poking some more and looking up.

"Twenty thousand dollars," he said. "Including the value of the tree."

Then everything got crystal clear. So I asked him flat out, "If we pay you twenty thousand, it'll move the road to the ridge?"

And he said, "Yes."

That was all we had to hear. I gathered up our maps and papers. We thanked Wucker for his time and took off.

We drove south without talking much because we were in shock. Judy said she'd caught a fever from the Federal Building, first getting hot and then going into shivers. A mixture of feelings boiled around inside me as we drove home. I was angry. I was feeling hopeless because by moving back into the hills, we'd run smack into the very thing we were trying to escape and I knew Judy was deep in thought about moving to Montana.

At the top of the canyon, just below the junction, we saw a man hitchhiking the opposite way and probably wouldn't have even noticed him at all except for the way he was dressed.

"Businessman hitchhiking," Judy said.

He was wearing a blue suit, standing in the snow with no hat. Although we didn't know at the time, it was Orrin McCutcheon, heading down to see Mitsy Thornbek. It was just about three o'clock by then.

We started up the dirt road to the cabin, finally relaxing as we entered the forest. When we came around the first corner, we spotted a camper tucked nose first into the trees like someone had accidentally run off the road and left it there. It had a bumper sticker that said *Camper Land* in silver letters. Of course, we didn't connect it with the man hitchhiking in the blue suit, not until the next morning, that is, when we found him laying stiff dead next to it.

"Look, Dean," Judy said. "Camper Land's all the way up here now."

"We're home. Don't worry," I said, but she just looked at me with her eyes wide like a cat. She had beads of sweat on her forehead.

We got home just before dark and started a fire and Judy laid down, first piling blankets on herself and shivering and then throwing them all off and sprawling out with her arms and legs hanging everywhere. The radio announced a winter storm warning for a big snow curling down from the Gulf of Alaska, starting the next night and going for two days, a real dumper that would no doubt shut the mountain down good.

Even though the storm came as a surprise, we were almost ready, having stored up a good amount of powdered milk and dry food to last a long winter. We had all the apples we could eat, picked fresh at Woodfords and stacked in bags and boxes in the root cellar. We needed more potatoes and winter squash and ammunition. We needed gasoline for the chain saw—a Stihl 036, dependable as a good dog—even though we had more than four cords already cut and stacked outside.

Nobody will ever know *exactly* what happened on the mountain that night. Judy fell asleep first and I stayed up, watching the fire. All of a sudden, Judy laughed out loud in her sleep, a big laugh that roared like fire in a woodstove. The cats woke up and looked at me. Then we all fell asleep.

From what I can piece together from the radio and also from talking to the bear hunters who'd read the newspapers and showed up at our cabin a few days later, Mr. McCutcheon stashed the camper, hitchhiked back down to Nevada, picked up Mitsy Thornbek, and took off in her green Toyota to get married at Lake Tahoe. When they got to the junction, he pulled over and probably told her he had to take a leak or something, so he walked around behind the car, slipped on his gloves, pulled a gun out of his pants and walked back to the window. But things didn't work out like he'd planned, judging from the amount of blood everywhere, not only inside the car but all over Orrin himself when we found him.

She must have turned around and spotted the gun a few seconds earlier than he figured, and being an old Nevada gal at heart, she did the natural thing by trying to grab the gun, which ended in her getting shot in the neck. According to the bear hunters, the bullet hit her vein and blood started spurting all over inside the car, pumping like it does. But Mitsy wasn't full dead and still had enough sense to realize she'd been double-crossed, so she grabbed on tight with one hand to the pillowcase full of money and used the other hand to latch on to Orrin until he fired the final shot to the side of her head. The coroner said that was about nine o'clock.

Orrin took the pillowcase and ran down the road toward the junction and then up the dirt road to the camper. Of course he was scared, just having botched a murder, covered with blood, which by then was cold and sticky, his heart crashing in his chest not only from running but from fright and the high altitude—over 7,500 feet. When he made it to the camper, he took off a glove, fumbled for his keys, and keeled over dead from a heart attack. We think that was the same time Judy laughed so loud in her sleep. It works out about right.

The next morning, like any morning, we woke up and had coffee in bed and played with the cats. A sheet of silver clouds rose up over the crest like a crown, the sign of coming snow. After filling the woodstove, we took off down the road toward the junction.

"Camper Land again," Judy said as we came around the corner. I slowed down and then stopped and Judy put her hands on her head. "Oh, Dean," she said, "look! It's the hitchhiking businessman laying down."

And there he was, laying on his side in his blue suit with one bare hand up in the air, covered with blood and a dusting of snow. He looked like a quarterback who'd just thrown a long pass and then suddenly frozen solid and tipped over. The keys were laying in the snow where he'd dropped them and his eyes were popped wide open, staring directly at the pillowcase, which also had blood on it. His shoes were shiny.

"We gotta get the sheriff," I said, and Judy said, "We can't just *leave* him here."

"It's a murder. We can't take him *with* us," I said, not knowing it was simply a heart attack and that the real murder was still sitting up the road in a green Toyota.

"You go get Duane," Judy said. "I'll stay here and keep the critters away."

By this time, *my* heart felt like it was ready to pop as I drove straight for the highway, not following the road but cutting directly through the trees and bouncing across the meadow. Although Duane wasn't much of a sheriff, he was all we had, and he lived just a mile away in a little subdivision by the river.

When we got back, Duane dropped down on his knees alongside the body.

"Where'd all this blood come from?" he asked me and Judy, like we already had the whole thing figured out. We shrugged our shoulders.

Then he opened the pillowcase and pulled out a handful of bundled cash.

"There's bunches of hundreds in here," he said. "Must be fifty grand." And his guess was good because there turned out to be sixty thousand in the pillowcase. He ran to his radio and before long there were more lights and uniforms than we'd ever seen on our road. About half an hour later somebody found Mitsy Thornbek sitting in her green Toyota and everything started making sense. The sky was flat gray and it was ready to snow. We could smell it.

By the time we got to town and loaded up the truck and made it back to the cabin, it was snowing hard. The sun had set and the wind picked up like a blizzard and big flakes piled up fast. While I unpacked the truck, Judy started a fire and when it warmed up, we started peeling off clothes.

Then Judy said, "Oh, look." She said it like she'd found her favorite hairbrush in an unexpected place as she pulled hundred-dollar bills out of her pants and piled them on the table. Thirty thousand dollars, to be exact.

"Jesus Christ," I said. "That's dead man money."

"Relax," she said. "It's survival of the fittest, like when a big animal eats a little animal."

"It ain't the same," I said. "The money's got numbers on it, Judy." Of course, that was before we talked to the bear hunters two days later.

"Oh, Dean," she said, like I was just being my old unreasonable self, taking a stand on *principle,* even though it didn't make much common sense. The way she had it figured, we'd stash the money until spring and then give Mr. Wucker twenty thousand to move the road. If nothing happened to Wucker, we'd save the Old Man *and* have ten thousand free and clear for the future. If Wucker got caught, he'd have a real tough time explaining where the money came from and we'd just move to Montana for a while.

"It's not the same in Montana," I said, and she said, "Montana's got mountains. Montana's got snow."

It snowed. It snowed an inch an hour all night, right on through the next day, and by the following morning we had almost four feet on the ground around us. To get out of the cabin, I had to push the door and pack the snow back enough to squeeze through. Winter changed everything.

It took about a week or so to settle down to an easy rhythm of sleeping and eating and hunting, or just sitting. Each thing we did—splitting a chunk of wood, fixing a window, or waiting for Orion to rise—everything made such plain and simple sense. Our hearts beat slower. Until the snow melted, we forgot the city and all the trouble it can bring, remembering only in our dreams the reasons why we have come so far to be alone. It felt like shedding a skin, like a snake does, leaving it behind like an old suitcase. Everything slowed down, almost like hibernation.

All morning we shoveled. We shoveled two paths to reach the things we needed most: one path to the outhouse and another path to the Old Man. When we finally reached him, we cleared an area around his trunk and rested. We sat on chunks of wood, watching the forest and telling stories, trying to give *reason* for things that had no reason at all, hoping to understand why people do the crazy things they do.

Judy told how she took the money, using a long pine limb to hook the pillowcase from a distance so she wouldn't leave footprints in the snow around it, using the same pine limb to lower the pillowcase back into its spot and then throwing snow in the air. "Like powdered sugar on a cake," she said.

The next day the bear hunters appeared out of nowhere. The two of them stood there without moving, each with a hound dog, like the whole bunch had simply dropped out of the sky and landed in the snow. Rifle barrels poked up over their shoulders, and each one held his dog by the collar so its front paws dangled off the ground. The dogs did not move or make noise, as if they were real accustomed to being choked. They stared in our direction, all four of them, sniffing the wind to catch our scent.

"Bear hunters," Judy whispered, because there was no mistaking them for what they were. "Oh, Dean, they're greasy."

They were six feet tall and looked like possums. Although they didn't have the sheen of grease, they did give the *feeling* of grease—animal grease, not car grease—with a glazed look in their eyes. The dogs' tails stuck straight out like arrows.

"Hey there," I said.

I had the feeling they were gauging us, carefully listening to the sound of my voice more than the words I was saying, watching us not directly like humans but more through the sides of their vision like some animals do.

"Heard about you," the first one said. "You're famous."

"Famous in my own family," I said, trying to make a joke. They didn't laugh.

We talked back and forth for a while, Judy staying stone quiet, which worried me because she's like a volcano that way, standing dormant and then all of a sudden blowing out a real whopper at the worst time. The bear hunters filled us in on the dead man story, some of which we'd heard on the radio. Then the other one said, "They say there's money missin'."

"Forty thousand," the first one added.

"Missin' where?" I said, but they just looked askance without moving their heads much, like they were looking for money tracks in the snow.

They told us how Mitsy Thornbek had withdrawn almost a hundred thousand dollars and that the police found out she had a little scheme of taking each withdrawal to the casinos and cashing it all in for gambling chips. Then she'd sit at the bar and waste some time before cashing the chips back in for different money so it couldn't be traced.

"A hundred minus sixty leaves forty," the one said.

And then Judy, of course, blew her cork and said, "Well, then you must be a fuckin' professor of mathematics and not a greasy-ass bear hunter at all."

The bear hunters didn't know what to say at first, especially as Judy was a woman and bear hunters know how to handle most anything that faces them except a woman like Judy. They looked back and forth, not really looking at each other or at anything at all until they left, turning the dogs loose and following them downslope toward the meadow, where they lingered for a long time, moving back and forth along the gray line of trees.

After dark, when the wind died and the snow pressed down heavy on the whole mountain, we heard one loud gunshot and the echo of a gunshot that seemed to fly up from the meadow and circle in the pines above our cabin. It was the last we heard of the bear hunters for a while, but we thought about them from time to time and wondered where they spent the night. Judy knew they'd be back.

"They smelled the money," she said more than once, as we slowly settled into our winter life, focusing down on fewer things, simple and understandable things. "They could tell by watching our fingers," she said. "They could see by our feet."

She started talking again about moving back to Montana, packing out on a sunny day by herself and heading straight cross-country for the highway. "The city's closin' in," she'd say. "I'm tired of it."

Less than a week later it snowed again, starting first as a freezing rain and then changing over, leaving an icy crust thick enough to walk on if you slid your feet just right. I went out hunting for anything—a deer, a squirrel, a big fat grouse—tracking along the creek until I broke into the chaparral on the open slopes below the old volcano. I hunkered against a boulder to get out of the wind, leaning back and looking over the whole country as if it belonged to me, as if, with two guns crossed in my lap, I could somehow claim the wilderness as my own. Then, out of the corner of my eye, I saw movement in a stand of aspen below the creek, so I lifted my .30-06 and looked through the scope, scanning along the line of trees.

I saw red, just a flash, and held my breath as if I'd seen the unmistakable color of my own blood: the red of their plaid hats, the two dogs, the skulking course they took over the snow. I watched the bear hunters and wondered why they had wandered so far in the snow again, although deep inside I knew. Not more than three hundred yards away, I could have dropped them like two deer under an apple tree. First one, then the other. Just like that. The dogs would have run and died their own deaths in a more natural way.

I hooked my finger around the trigger and held my breath, steadying the scope, studying their movement, trying to read the meaning of their crazy gestures. Like animals they moved, stopping for no apparent reason, backtracking, splitting apart and coming together by the creek, always staying downwind of the cabin. I raised my sight right over their heads to the far slopes of the crest, resting the crosshairs gently on the horizon. I imagined them below me, unaware and whispering. Then I pulled the trigger.

They skittered across the snow. A few times they broke through the crust because they were not concentrating on sliding their feet as they disappeared into the forest. That was the last time I saw them, but I still think of them.

When I got back to the cabin, Judy sat cross-legged on the floor in front of the woodstove, holding both cats at once and looking at me with big eyes. I told her the shot I'd fired just missed the biggest buck on the whole mountain. She knew I was lying, so I described the buck in greater detail, hoping it would convince her my story was true, but it didn't.

"It was *them,* wasn't it?" she said.

"No."

Then something strange happened. Just after sunset a

few days later, we were in the cabin relaxing after dinner. We had a good fire going because another storm was coming, the wind already blowing and rattling the glass in our window. Judy jumped into bed, buried herself under the comforter and started throwing her clothes all over the room until she was buck naked. She smiled a beautiful warm and inviting smile. I did a little dance around the floor, a kind of courtship dance but also somewhat kooky because she laughed as I undressed and strutted back and forth in the lamplight with my thumbs under my arms like a game bird.

I tumbled into bed. Our flesh melted together—it really did—our arms and legs stirring like currents in a creek. As always, we had all the time in the world, time for everything. Time to do things right, without mistakes. Time to think. And endless time—all the days and nights and days until the earth pushed up through the snow again—to kiss. We forgot completely, for a while, where we were and even *who* we were until Judy's body suddenly stiffened and I raised my head to look at her.

"What was that?" she said.

"What was *what*?"

"That sound. Outside."

I jumped out of bed, grabbed the shotgun, pushed open the door and stood there stark naked, pointing into the wilderness. Nothing. Nothing but the big open maw of the mountain in the last moment before darkness, when familiar things lose their color and shape so that everything points in all directions at once and looks like nothing at all. I closed the door and rolled back into bed.

In the short time before we fell asleep, we held each other and talked in whispers about little things we had done that day. I put a large chunk of wood in the fire and we listened to it snap and pop as it started to burn. I pulled Judy closer, cupping my hand around her strong shoulder, and we shared a vision of the future. We pictured the meadow and the lake when springtime finally climbs the mountain and ducks and geese come sailing in. We imagined the sweet smell of Jeffrey pine, warmed by an afternoon sun, until the aroma filled the cabin. One by one, we named the flowers that signal the end of winter: the lupine and paintbrush and mule's ear in the chaparral above us, wild rose and penny-royal along the creek, the rare and beautiful shooting star. But these were winter dreams and we had all the time in the world for dreaming.

We snuggled closer together and Judy rested her head on my chest. She listened to my heart. I could feel it beating and I could feel her heart, too, with my hand. We laid there for a while without talking and without moving, listening, and listening to the wind whipping around the cabin, drifting another layer of snow that would push us even further from spring. As we closed our eyes and our breathing became more measured, our hearts slowed down together, beating slowly, but definitely, like one large heart pulsing just a few times a minute. We curled up once more against each other, comfortable, a little frightened and a little reassured, like two bears on the soft edge of sleep.

FLYING TO THE MOON

Froggy had the job of chasing mushroom clouds in a Plymouth Fury. Before that, he flew after them in airplanes until he started having dizzy spells and blacking out, so they grounded him and gave him the Fury, but that was before I knew him. I guess they figured he'd do a lot less damage if he simply crashed a car in the sagebrush rather than going down in a whole plane full of people.

Even though I'd never really seen one of his dizzy spells until the day I drove with him, I made the mistake of telling my folks about them and about the fact that Froggy thought he was going to the moon. Of course, they grounded me from driving with him, but like Froggy said when he picked me up before sunrise the next day and we took off for Yucca Flat to watch the biggest bomb blast in Nevada history, "Buddy," he said—he always called me Buddy, even though my name was Jason—"Buddy, you and me got a solid bond. We both been grounded, but we're destined for greater things." Although he never told me exactly what those *greater things* were, I believed him. It was 1962 and I was seventeen. John Glenn had just blasted into orbit a few months before, and I had a picture of him and a picture of Froggy on my bedroom wall.

When I hopped in the car that morning, Froggy waited for the cigarette lighter to pop and then took his foot off the brake.

"Pilot to Navigator," he said, talking into his fist. Early in the morning his voice was even froggier than usual, which is how he got his name, although he did have the lips of a frog, and the eyes and the smooth skin.

"Navigator," I said.

"Prepare for takeoff."

I grabbed his thermos as all those hundreds of horses stampeded under the hood. It was a big car, built for speed and the long haul, highly chromed with curved fenders and specially tinted windows and enough room inside for two families. Froggy slipped the shifter straight into overdrive, and I felt myself sink back into the huge seat cushion as we took off south for Yucca Flat.

At least once a month Froggy would roll into our place and tell us about a bomb blast about to happen. That was his job. He'd tell us the day and the name of the blast, names like Shot Smoky or Shot Priscilla or Shot Dirty Harry, and he'd give us film badges to measure fallout, but we never wore them. I always thought Froggy was a normal guy, just like the rest of us. My father didn't see it so. He said you can't trust a man whose only connection with the land was where his tires touched the road. But we'd talk sometimes, me and Froggy, about outer space and going to the moon. That was Froggy's dream. "Someday we'll fly there," he'd say. "You and me, Buddy." I believed him because he talked as if he *knew* it, like he was actually seeing it happen while he was talking, and I felt like all I'd have to do would be to go along for the ride. Back then, it was like all of us Americans were a family and President Kennedy was the father and we were loading up the car and driving to a better place.

Froggy drove the Plymouth like a plane, both hands on the wheel, always watching the gauges and checking his wristwatch, and we landed on a little mesa outside Mercury just before dawn. It gave us a straight-shot view of the whole valley. A big moon rose up, and all the yuccas stood like soldiers with their arms out, leaning together toward Las Vegas.

"T minus five minutes," Froggy said, tapping the crystal of his watch. He lit another cigarette from the one he was smoking, the whole car swirling with smoke, and it didn't bother me a bit because there was no such thing as secondhand smoke in those days.

You can see movies about atomic bombs going off. People try to describe it, but it's nothing like seeing one yourself, being right there. First came the light, like a thousand flashbulbs going off right in my eyes, and then the heat and the shock wave, which rocked the car like we were driving through a creek bed. After that, the wind and the sand blocked everything out like a blizzard until the light faded and the sky went deep, deep red. The fireball climbed straight up and turned every color of the rainbow—red and blue and yellow and green—the whole sky above us. One minute it was crystal clear, just a few stars and a big, grinning moon. Then there was only fire.

"Jesus," Froggy said. That's all he said as he circled the Fury and we took off toward Mercury to get some distance and see which way the cloud would carry. "Jesus Christ," he kept saying, as if the bomb had sucked all the other words in the whole language away for a while. I felt sick to my stomach.

"I wanna go home, Froggy," I whispered, not because I

was trying to be quiet, but the words just slipped out with my breath.

"Pilot to Navigator," he said, but I couldn't answer.

By the time we got to Mercury, the cloud had turned the whole sky pink. Froggy tapped the floating compass on the dashboard and we were off, a hundred miles an hour up the highway. The cloud didn't travel all that fast, but it blew with the wind over places with no roads, so we had to cut it off and stay with it, relying on the Fury for speed.

Only part of the job was tracking. The other part was passing out film badges and coming back to pick them up after the whole thing was over. In the backseat, Froggy kept a shopping bag full of film badges, which were made of heavy white paper about the size of a silver dollar with a safety pin on the back so you could fix it to your shirt. They measured fallout, but nobody knew if they worked, not even Froggy. He was supposed to give them to people or stick them on fence posts in front of schools and churches and brothels. But Froggy didn't pass too many out or pick many up because he mostly liked driving fast, so the badges he turned back to the Test Site came straight out of the bag in the backseat.

As we raced across Six Mile Valley, the cloud behaved like most clouds, heading straight for Saint George and Cedar City. That's when Froggy started acting strange. Right in the middle of nowhere, he turned onto the dirt road heading for the ghost town of Delamar. He drove fast, and the Fury swerved and scraped the sagebrush. Froggy's eyes were swimming in circles. It was the first time I'd ever seen one of his dizzy spells. Without slowing down, he dipped his head forward and looked out over the steering wheel like he was aiming the car across the valley.

"Froggy?" I said. "You all right?"

"A-OK." He looked at me, but turned away because he was

embarrassed about his eyes, which were moving around opposite of each other, slow and circular like they'd come disconnected.

"If you're gonna black out, I can drive." I was scared, even though we were out in the middle of nowhere with nothing to hit but sagebrush.

"This is jus' a little *vertigo,* like bein' lightheaded. Ain't you ever been lightheaded before?"

"Yeah. But not like that, with the eyes."

"The eyes jus' *looks* bad," he said. "I'm seein' twenty-twenty. Don't worry about it." But I did. I worried real bad.

We climbed out of the valley and broke into a meadow surrounded by rocky hills where the road flattened as Delamar rose up like old fingers between the trees. All the buildings were brown and weathered, all the ones still standing, that is, because so many had already fallen into heaps of tin and lumber or been hauled away board by board to build new ghost towns somewhere else. We stopped in the middle of town. Froggy got out of the car and sat down cross-legged in the street, closing his eyes and slumping forward with his hands on the sides of his head like he was trying to keep it from breaking apart. Then he shrugged his shoulders and laughed like he'd just heard a joke, and fell over flat back in the dirt, blacked out.

Like a bag of water, my stomach dropped out with the thought of being stuck in Delamar with a dead Froggy. But his lips moved as if he was talking, and his hands fluttered in the dirt at his sides. I felt completely alone. I tried to stand up, but the earth kept shifting under me and I lost all idea of time, not only of the hour that day but of the difference between that day and the day before and all the days ahead and the years behind. Then all of a sudden Froggy's eyes popped open and he sat right up.

"Whew!" he said. "That was a bad one." His eyes focused

on me, steady as two wet stones. Without saying a word, we got back in the Plymouth and took off. When we were well past the meadow and moving through the belly of the valley, he took a deep breath and sighed like he wanted to say something.

"Don't tell nobody what you seen," he said. "They'll take my car away. When a man can't drive his car anymore, it's emasculating. It makes you mad."

"Don't worry, Froggy," I said. "They won't take the car," even though I knew he didn't belong behind the wheel.

We hit the highway heading for Hiko. As we picked up speed, I sunk back into the big seat cushions of the Fury and rolled my window down. Froggy hooked his thumbs over the bottom of the steering wheel like he didn't much care which way we went. The speedometer topped a hundred miles an hour, the wind thumping through my window and the country flashing by in a blur of sagebrush and hills and sky, not only because we were going fast but also because my eyes were full of tears from the wind and the dust and from all that'd happened that day.

The Plymouth shimmied as we hit a hundred and fifteen, and the front end raised up like a plane on a runway. Above the hills straight in front of us, the full moon hung pale and milky in the morning sky. I felt weightless. Froggy smiled and grabbed a big handful of film badges from the shopping bag in the backseat, pushing his arm out the window and letting the badges fly between his fingers, like flower petals swirling behind us. And then, while both of us kept our eyes locked on the moon in the windshield, we left the Earth and flew together for a good distance in that direction.

Although the road curved to the left, Froggy drove straight. He still had his thumbs hooked on the steering wheel when we hit the berm on the side of the road and took off. It was a good-sized mound of dirt and would have been tough to drive over at twenty miles an hour, but at a hundred and twenty it was only a bump, like the little thump you feel just before leaving the ground in a jet plane. As we flew into the open arms of the moon, it seemed like a dream in which everything slows down, until our front end dipped and we banked left.

It was a rough landing because we were off balance, which caused us to tumble end over end. When we finally stopped, we were upside down, having been thrown all over inside because we didn't wear seat belts in those days, and there was a lot of blood mixed with glass and radiator fluid and steam, everything dripping down like rain. Froggy was curled up like a baby on the ceiling of the Plymouth, his hair all wet and plastered down, his arms and legs pointing in every direction at once. For a moment, he opened his eyes and looked at me. His hands fluttered like little wings, and he puckered his lips as if saying the word *moooon.* Then we both passed out. They found us an hour later.

What happened next was very strange. Froggy disappeared. He got banged up worse than me and no doubt hobbled around somewhere for a few months, but I never saw him or heard from him for seven years. Some folks said he'd gone down south to Pahrump with his mother. Others said he'd moved to Utah. Because he worked for the government, everything was fairly hush-hush.

Seven years is a long time and it's a short time. A lot happened in the time before I saw Froggy again. My father died of leukemia, his white blood cells spooked into a wild stampede by the constant wiggling of some tiny nematode, leaving me in the saddle of his sagebrush empire. I married my girlfriend, Lorna, and we had three children—Valerie, Vern, and Varlin—the seeds of my greatness, the carriers of my hope for a world where honesty and fairness prevail. To hope for less—to send them riding into a country where there is no payoff for a hard day's work—would be unthinkable. And at the tail end of those seven years, Neil Armstrong walked on the moon just like President Kennedy had predicted.

On the day of the moonwalk—July 23, 1969—I wondered if Froggy was still alive, and what he thought about this landing on the moon. I wondered if, like me, he felt somehow disappointed, not because the astronauts had finally made it and we had failed, but because the moon was suddenly no longer what it always had been. Ever since Indian times, people had watched the moon climb into the sky at night, imagining all sorts of things to explain the course it took, its changing shape, or the size and color it seemed to have. The dream was over. My sense of wonder was gone, reduced, like the moon itself, to a string of snapshots—a starched American flag planted like a real estate sign in the desert, the giant step of a puffy moon boot, a golf swing in a silent movie. Seven years is really not much time at all.

A week after the moonwalk I saw Froggy again, during a trip to Cedar City for supplies. I walked into Great Basin Hardware, my last stop on the western edge of town before the long haul home. That's where I saw him, dressed in the orange-and-blue uniform of that old store, standing in the plumbing aisle with a drainpipe in both hands, explaining the science of water flow to an old woman. I kept walking. I knew it was him, even though he'd weathered a good amount and lost a lot of weight. He looked haggard and hooked, like a hungry buzzard. For a few minutes, I wandered around the store, wondering if I should talk to him. I passed the plumbing aisle again, quickly, moving on like a spy. His voice was froggier than ever.

I paid for my things and left the store, laughing out loud as I drove out of the parking lot onto the road leading back to my wife and children, our small house and uncertain future.

Froggy and I had never been destined for great things at all. Like most folks, we gently surrendered to the steady pull of gravity and did not realize that desire and perseverance and blind luck are sometimes not enough to overcome such force.

From the eastern hills, a big, grinning moon swelled into the sky like a ripe fruit. I picked out Froggy's pale features: his thin lips and withered skin, his lidless eyes. I wondered what Froggy feared. I wondered what he hoped for the most now.

When I got home, Lorna was waiting for me on the front porch, standing in the moonlight, arms open, wearing the blue nightgown that I love. She gave me a good, long hug, the kind that lets you know you've really been missed, and I held her like she was the last thing on Earth. We looked across the yard, past the silvery fields of fresh alfalfa and deep into the darkness beyond. I pressed my lips against the crown of her head. Without moving and without speaking, we listened to the sounds of that summer night—a few crickets, the rustle of dry grass in a balmy breeze, the lowing of a lone cow somewhere out of sight—the whole thing brushing against us like a fine and gentle fabric. It was peaceful. It felt so right, so perfectly correct and satisfying, as if everything I'd ever done—every blunder and false assumption, every good decision—had somehow culminated in this one clear moment.

X

When the great gray owl showed up during a snowstorm, he was the size of a small boy. An owl that hangs around a certain place for a while has usually made up its mind to kill. My brothers started wearing big hats to protect themselves and to distract the owl, and they locked all the doors and windows. It was entertaining.

On Saturday morning, I got a call from my friend David, who said he needed me to keep him company. I ran to meet him at the corner, and that owl skimmed the top of my head and knocked my hat off. David liked having me around. I told him where to go and how much money to spend on me. He didn't mind. He liked the attention. I would always touch him adoringly on the face.

That night, David and I went to a dance and he told me he loved me. We love to dance. Afterward, we went to a park covered in snow with a big gazebo in the middle. It was past midnight. We danced in the gazebo to music from his car radio and he asked me to be his. I kissed him hard and said no. The next day he tried to kill himself.

The owl sat in front of my house. The next night, as I

watched from my bedroom window and the owl shifted from foot to foot, dancing on the wire, a car came down the street and flashed its lights at me. I carefully opened my bedroom window and slipped out, trying not to wake my father. It was my friend Babs. She looked wild. Her hair was blown back by the wind and her small round glasses were not on her face. She was crying and asked me to come with her. I thought something had happened. She was just lonely.

We drove to the water tank and climbed to the top. It was cold there and I told her about the owl, how it had a personality.

"Oh, no," she said. "There's just owls—owls that grow up to be owls. Just plain owls."

She was so sexual. Her movements were wispy and feathery. I loved being with her, no matter what we did. She tried to kiss me, but I turned away and told her I was a waste for her because my counselor told me I had low self-esteem. Babs started crying again.

In the morning the owl left for a few hours. I slept until noon. David said I was acting peculiar. He always had remedies for my discontent. That afternoon, he got me so drunk I threw up on him and he still caressed my back while I heaved up vomit. We drove around in his ugly car and did opium in front of a church. A police officer came and took me away from him because he was a known character and they didn't want me around him. I cried in the police car and threw a bottle of shampoo at my father when I got home. After that, I had to coax David to go places with me, telling him there would be good drugs, food, or music. He said people don't understand him and that all his friends, including me, gave up on him.

But the owl was there every day and every night. He was even there the night the ambulance came to the house next door. The whole neighborhood woke up and lights went on because people wanted to know what had happened. There were a lot of weird noises, and I never found out why the ambulance came, or if anyone was hurt or ill. Everything was very hush-hush.

Right out of the blue, Babs fell in love with Adrian because he gave her flowers. He was a Washoe Indian from the edge of town where the speed limit is 15 mph. They decided to get married and she insisted their child should be Catholic.

"Why Catholic?" I asked her.

"I don't know," she said. "But I'll wear black if it's an Indian wedding."

We were at my house, peeking at the owl. All of a sudden, the neighbor's sheep called Babs's name. *Baaaaaabs.*

A few days later, the snow melted completely and the owl disappeared, just as suddenly and smoothly as he had come. Although seeing an owl is rare, especially in the middle of our valley, I watched for him. Owls can live fifteen years.

That night, as I lay in bed, I thought I heard my father walking around the house when everybody should have been sleeping. The floor creaked as he moved from room to room. The creaking—back and forth—I figured it might have been the house settling. It could have been anything.

CLOUDSHINE

It was hot. It was the hottest summer I ever saw, the whole country just waiting to pop or simply bust into flames. From the porch I watched Jason ride over the alfalfa and through the tall weeds along the ditch, where he stopped and slumped in the saddle. His head rolled back and he looked straight up to the sky and put his arms out like he was feeling for rain, which there wasn't any of. When his arms started going like he was leading a symphony, I knew there was trouble and I could hear him yelling, but not the words he was saying. Then he took off at a full run along the dirt road around the orchard and straight toward Murray Stichell's place, just whipping that horse over and under and kicking up a cloud of dust.

For a minute, Kay stopped the tractor and watched him, wondering, no doubt, what Jason would do *this* time, because it wasn't the first time Murray'd helped himself to something that wasn't entirely his own. Kay knew he'd been stealing water ever since late the night before, when he walked out among the tall weeds with a flashlight and a shovel, not because he needed to be there in the pitch of night, but because the pain wouldn't let him sleep. "Somebody's takin' water," he said as he got back to bed, but he didn't say *who* and he didn't tell Jason the next morning.

Kay quit plowing and came in to lay on the couch, which is the way it was back then. He'd wake up and get working on a project, but after a couple hours he'd get tired and lay down the rest of the day. When he came through the door that morning, he never left the house again in the weeks he had left.

"White blood cells stampeding," he said, which is how he explained the chronic leukemia that was killing him. He was a cowboy clean to the bone and used the only words he knew to let me know how he felt. "It's a heavy pain," he'd say, or, "the cells are all corralled in my neck," or, "feels like I got lumpy jaw," which is a cow disease.

Jason was my youngest son, from my first husband who died of cancer. All Kay's children from his first wife, who also died, grew up and moved on like mine, gone to Salt Lake City and Las Vegas to work on computers and business and such. But Jason had just turned twenty-five and it looked like he was going to stick around, which he did, even though he was the worst one growing up and never did get along with Kay or call him dad, like the older ones had.

He marched in and sat down next to the bed.

"There's a problem, Kay," he said. "Murray's stealin' water again."

"Oh?" Kay just puckered his lips and looked at his hands. "You run into Murray?"

"He seen me shut his gates and I waved at him, kinda."

"Kinda?" Kay looked up and scratched his jaw.

"Well, I sorta shook my fist at him, but he was far away."

That was a big deal. It was big not only because folks in

Hiko didn't often shake their fists at each other, not in plain view anyway, but also because Murray Stichell was the bishop of our ward, which in the Mormon Church is the spiritual leader of a whole area, and although our ward was few in people, it was large in country, taking in all of Hiko and Warm Springs and stretching all the way to the Test Site and over to Adaven.

"What'd Murray do when you showed'm your fist?" Kay asked.

"He waved back. Waved and then prophesied. Told me not to worry about water 'cuz rain was comin' real soon."

Murray Stichell was more than just a neighbor and he was more than just a bishop. And the reason Kay let Murray get away with so much was not only that Kay was the one person I've ever known to be the most like Jesus Christ, being tolerant and forgiving and kindhearted, but also that Kay was beholden to Murray because Murray's grandfather went to World War I in Kay's grandfather's place. It happened that Kay's grandfather couldn't go to the war because his own father had died and he ran the farm with his mother and his younger brother, who most likely had some mental problem, but folks just called him *dumb* in those days. And so started a tradition between families that began as a righteous repaying of an unselfish deed, but which got corrupted over time. Like their fathers before them, Kay grew up a giver and Murray grew up a borrower, whether it came to shovels or tractors or diesel fuel, and it'd gone on for so long there was just no explaining it and no easy way to back out of it.

Although Jason was raised in it, he never accepted it as his own, mostly because he wasn't the blood son of Kay and partially because he was so willful to begin with. When the drought hit and Murray added *water* to the list of things he simply took when he got the notion, he hadn't fully reckoned that Kay'd be dead by the first of August, it already being the middle of July, and that Jason would be running the place in our name.

Less than an hour after the fist-shaking, Murray drove up our road in his old truck and parked near the shop under the cottonwood tree. We all figured he'd come to borrow something, but instead he started *unloading* his truck of things he'd already borrowed. He hauled out a shovel and a digging bar, a few hand tools and a saddle, which he slung over a sawhorse. He knew we were watching him.

"Something had to be done," Jason said, as if his fist-shaking had turned Murray around and stemmed the tide of generations. Murray sat in his truck and rubbed his thighs like he did when he was thinking. It was a habit of his. All his jeans were worn light on the legs around the pockets because he did so much rubbing and so much thinking, and, according to Jason, so little working. There was no door on his truck, and folks got used to seeing him driving down the road in plain view like that. It's funny to see somebody driving a truck when you can see him from head to foot. Around the shop he went, driving with one hand and thinking with the other. It was hot. Although water kept gushing out of the ground at the Hiko spring, it didn't rain that day or the next day or any day in the next weeks like Murray had prophesied. Every morning the sun came up in the same spot and cooked us dry, and the flies were bad. There wasn't a cloud in the sky. It was the worst summer for flies I ever saw.

Kay went down fast and died on the last day of July. It wasn't a week before Jason had run head-to-head with Murray Stichell again, over water, of course. I tried to stop him. I explained how these things have a way of growing into feuds with a mind of their own, that we'd have to face Murray every Sunday in church, and that he was our bishop. But before the week was up he started, sometimes before dawn and when he knew Murray wasn't around, digging a new ditch to bypass Stichell's place altogether.

He dug by hand with a bar and a shovel, carving out a gully two feet wide and two feet deep, starting back behind the boneyard and hugging the toe of the hill. It was slow going, very rocky. By the time he'd reached the old orchard, his back acted up and he started taking pills. He came in one morning for breakfast, already dirty and tired, swallowing four pills at a time with his orange juice and cussing Murray more out of habit than anything else.

"This is stupid," he said. "It's hurtin' me." And without looking up from his food he said, "I'm gonna sue him," which was the first time in my life I ever heard a person in Hiko threaten to sue another person.

"You can't sue Murray," I said. "Why don't you knock on his door?"

"I done that last week," he said. "I knocked and he come out and said the gates musta busted open by themself and that he'd go right out and close 'em up, but he already *got* all the water he needed. And the gates didn't just bust open because I saw 'em laid up on the ditch behind. Ol' Murray hopped in his truck with no door and I seen him drivin' along the ditch with one hand and rubbin' his leg with the other, thinkin' real hard how he got away with half a day of water and how he'd get away again."

The next day Jason drove all the way to Caliente to find a lawyer. I was in between a rock and a hard place, being the proper owner of the farm and the mother of Jason, who was really the *man* of the outfit, as he knew how to run the place more than me. And on the other hand was Murray, the lifelong friend of Kay and a simple and gentle man at heart, but Lord knows how quick people change when they feel like they're trapped in a corner. Jason had his mind made up, and there wasn't a thing I could say to sway him. Like his real father, he was strong-willed and hotheaded, and five years of drought had slowly boiled out the best in him—boiled out the best in everybody.

Before noon he was back. He'd talked to the only three lawyers in the whole county, and not one of them would take the case of a church member against his own bishop. So Jason turned to Las Vegas and found Trudy Silverglide, who charged us five hundred dollars to drive up in her little red sports car, eat lunch, and take a few pictures. Five hundred dollars.

"That's five ton of hay," I told Jason after she'd left.

"It's a small price to pay. It's the *principle.*"

"Principle," I said. "Ha!"

How do you tell a twenty-five-year-old that *principle* is not such an important thing? How do you explain that there are other things, like having to live in a community and get along well enough to survive and carry on? I was afraid. I didn't know what to do.

The letter wasn't supposed to be mailed to Murray until we had a chance to approve, but it went out anyway, by mistake. Trudy Silverglide had her own reasons, I'm sure, to mail the letter, and they weren't the same reasons Jason had. I asked him what good on God's green earth he figured would come of it, besides poisoning the very water we were trying to protect. He just shrugged his shoulders. "Principle," he said. But we were already a long way past *principle.* It just goes to show that sometimes big things that upset or drag down whole communities of hardworking people can happen by mistake, by accident, or for reasons crossways to the ones we believe.

All week long there was a kind of cloud that settled in Hiko Valley, not a cloud you could see—the sun still baked us bone dry and seemed to suck every drop of moisture and energy out of us from the time we opened our eyes in the morning—but rather a cloud you could feel. It put me in mind of the pinkish and pretty clouds that rolled into Hiko Valley during the days of the atomic bomb blasts, back when I first met Kay, in the summer of 1957. They'd stay for a day or two sometimes, depending on the wind, and they weren't like clouds at all, not like big billowy clouds that move with the wind or bring rain, and not exactly like a fog either, so the kids called it *cloudshine,* and the name stuck.

Cloudshine had taste, like a salty metal in your mouth, and it had the tingly feel of electricity. The new cloud certainly had bad taste, and it carried the feeling of electricity as it made the hairs stand up on my arms and burned the back of my neck like a small sunburn. It was quiet. Four days later we got a letter from the Forest Service, breaking the silence and telling us that we were in trespass on government land and although the letter came all the way from Reno, I knew it had roots in Murray Stichell. Nobody except Murray even knew about the little log cabin we'd built.

You have to go clear out to Coal Valley and follow a two-track dirt road another nineteen miles through the black sage, into the juniper and piñon pine. A little spur road cuts off to Cottonwood Creek, another fifteen minutes to the cabin. We built it of Jeffrey pine cut from further up the hill and dragged down with Murray's own tractor, with Murray himself in the driver's seat. A whole summer it took us, me and Kay and Jason mainly, when we had an extra day or two, and we slept in the sheep wagon or under the stars by the creek when it was warm.

The Forest Service gave us thirty days to remove the "living structure" or they would remove it and bill us for "all costs, plus a 25% administrative fee," which meant they'd torch the cabin and we'd pay for everything including the matches and the postage stamp on the letter they'd send us telling us the cabin wasn't there anymore. I broke down and cried. Being a woman, I could only do so much, and Jason ran the ranch just fine, but he was young and somewhat hotheaded when it came to having good judgment or knowing just where he stood among the generations.

"We'll take it apart log by log," he said. "Chunk it up for firewood and have it down and out in a day."

"I'm not a young lady anymore," I said.

"Then come and watch me."

We did the chores and hit the road at sunup, bouncing through Coal Valley in the big white truck with the windows down because it was already warm. Dust filtered up through the floorboards, settling on everything, shifting around like a fine mist. By the time we got to the cabin, it was already hot. We stood in the shade of the cottonwoods and looked at the creek, which didn't have any water in it for the first time I ever knew. It just wasn't the same without the creek, without the sound of water and the birds that come. The trees were pale and wilted, and the whole place had lost its feeling of homeyness.

Jason crossed his arms on his chest and squinted at the cabin as if trying to look right through it and remember exactly how the whole thing was attached and how it would come apart. It was a just another job to him, with a beginning and an end, completely disconnected from anything that came before it or would come after.

"Piece a cake," he said. "I'll put a wedge cut in the post, wrap the chain around, and pull it down with the truck." Except we didn't need the truck or the chain because Jason did such a good job with the wedge cut, he nearly killed himself.

He went to work on the main post with the chain saw, filling the cabin with smoke and noise, wood chips flying. It was sad to see the cabin go, especially the *way* it was going and for the *reason* it was going, and I started feeling a little sick to my stomach and a little dizzy and then I thought I was losing my balance because the cabin shifted and it felt like I was falling, but I wasn't. Jason cut too far through the post and the whole roof started to shift, the little cabin only held together with mud and gravity to begin with. By the time he knew what was happening, it was too late. The roof came down and pulled two walls with it. I thought for sure he was killed or crushed bad, but when I called him he answered.

"I got it down!" he yelled from inside. "Get me outta here!"

I crawled up to the spot where his voice came out and I could see his red shirt through a hole about the size of my hand, but he was a long way in there.

"My foot's hurt," he said. And then, "Put the chain around the logs and pull 'em off with the truck," even though he *knew* that wasn't the way to do it. It needed a backhoe to *lift* the logs rather than simply dragging them and upsetting the whole pile and squashing him.

"I'll have to get help," I said. I told him I'd drive as fast as I could, and just before I closed the truck door, I heard him call.

"Hey, Mom! Whatever you do, don't get Murray!" But he knew Murray owned the only backhoe in Hiko.

When I pulled into Stichell's place, I saw Murray's legs sticking out from inside his baler, wavering like feelers on a big bug. He was waist deep in machinery, squirming and fighting at something, and he backed out when he heard the truck. I was nervous. Even though I'd seen him a few times in town and at church, we hadn't talked since Kay's funeral, and he had a scared look on his face, like he was afraid to see me.

"What's wrong with Jason?" he said, just like that, like he knew what'd happened without me saying a word.

"The cabin's fell on him," I said, and I told him the story. While I was telling him, he was rubbing his legs with both hands, thinking fast and furious and wiping grease off and before I was done telling, he'd already dragged two heavy chains from the shop and piled them on the floorboards of his truck, which he backed up to a flatbed and loaded the backhoe, and we were off.

Murray felt bad. I could tell with the way he kept saying, "I hope he ain't hurt serious" every time there was a silence, which there wasn't too much of on account of his truck, which made more noise than any truck I ever rode in.

"It's just his foot," I'd say. But Murray felt personally responsible for everything that happened.

"It was a good little cabin," he said. "I didn't wanna see it tore down. It's just I ain't never been sued before."

"You're not sued," I said.

He sat there with both hands on the wheel, staring straight ahead into the valley and said, "Bonnie, if Jason woulda been Kay's and your blood son, would all this not've happened?"

"I don't know." I didn't know for sure. But *something* upset the flow of generations, something that moved like a mouse without shaking the grass and left us to carry on as we could. Maybe it's just progress and modern times, the dying off of an old and useless way of life. Maybe it's something in the water that poisoned us from within, or the bone-dry end of a five-year drought that boiled out the best in all of us. I don't know.

Once we reached the cabin, Murray had Jason free inside of thirty minutes. His ankle was broken bad, bent square over from the rest of his leg. We drove to the hospital in Tonopah, another hour and a half, with him laying in the back of the truck on a bed of hay we made. Until we hit the highway it was a bumpy ride, and I could see by his face that he was going from being scared to being more angry as time went on and he came to know the fix he was in.

For two days he stayed in the hospital because they had to operate and put the bone back with screws and steel plates. When I brought him home, Murray's truck with no door was parked up by the corrals, and we spotted Murray himself doing the evening feeding. I got Jason into bed and went up to help Murray. That's when he had his largest prophecy and the last one of his life. As I came across the little bridge over the ditch, he stood there rubbing his legs real slow, looking at me like he was seeing me for the first time, his eyes swimming around in his head.

"The Lord works by revelation, Bonnie," he said. "I had the most revealin' dream last night, and today the whole world's upside down."

"You okay?" I said, because he'd prophesied a bunch before, but never like that, with the eyes wandering and his face flushed.

"It was a dream of great detail, covering all things that have ever been or ever will be, starting from the foundation of the world to the end." He swept his arm around as far as he could without turning. Then he looked up into the empty sky and said, "Ostriches."

"Sit down, Murray," I said, and I helped him onto a bale of hay and sat next to him with my arm around his shoulders.

"I never seen an ostrich in real life, but in my dream I seen 'em clear as day, long-legged critters with big, curious eyes. They was behind a chain-link fence in the middle of an alfalfa field. I was standin' outside the fence, and this big one come up and hooked his neck over the fence real slow and started peckin' at the brass button on my sleeve, lookin' at it and peckin' like it was somethin' real special. Then all of a sudden the big birds started a stampede 'round the corral like a herd, and the clouds come. They was big, heavy rain clouds that moved into the valley, coverin' the sun and lettin' down a drenchin' rain which lasted for six days, on and off."

At that point he tried to stand up, but he wobbled and put his arms out, so I helped him sit back down.

"Why ostriches?" I said.

"Don't know." He started to cry. He put his hands on the sides of his head and just whimpered. "I don't know where the ostriches come from," he said, "but it's the rain what's important as revelation. It was a washing rain at the end of a long dearth as we're now havin' because folks began to cry unto the Lord and humble themselves a good amount. So it's gonna rain real soon." He looked up with small tears rolling down his face, holding his head like he was trying to keep it from breaking apart. "The Lord knows we been humbled a good amount."

"Murray," I said, "what's the matter?"

And he said, "It's my head. Been hurtin' and everything's just spinnin'."

"How long's it been going on?"

"Couple'a months," he said. "Maybe little more."

"Prophecy is too hard work," I told him, and he smiled.

We sat there on a hay bale by the silo with the cows and horses lined up along the feeding trough. It was hot, and we smelled the sweet smell of hay and horses and heard the yellow birds that move through Hiko every year at that time. They flew in all of a sudden and ringed the top rail of the corral like candle flames. We didn't talk, but I knew we were both thinking about all that'd happened and about what was left of us to carry on. We sat there until the animals finished eating and started moving around again and Murray's head felt better. Then he got into his truck with no door and drove home. I still laugh out loud when I think of him in that truck, just rolling along with no door like everything was so perfectly normal.

Two days later he died, of a fast-growing brain tumor. He must not've been too dizzy to open his gates and take what he needed because when me and Jason crossed the irrigation ditch there was no water even though it was our week for water. Jason just shrugged his shoulders.

"Somebody's takin' water," he said. He looked up toward Murray's place and cried out, "Hey, Murray!" but of course Murray couldn't hear him, so he pressed his lips together and kept riding. That was a miracle. Funny how young people can change so fast. One day they decide to up and go off in some new direction, just like that. There they go. Another miracle was that it rained the next day. We must have been humbled a very good amount, because it rained real hard for six straight days, on and off, just like Murray prophesied, and it's kept raining regular for fifteen years now without a drought, and without my really knowing what upset the generations and why everything went upside down for us that summer.